D0933949

THE LONG SKELETON

The Long Skeleton

A Mr. and Mrs. North Mystery

BY

FRANCES AND RICHARD
LOCKRIDGE

J. B. LIPPINCOTT COMPANY
Philadelphia *New York*

PRINTED IN THE
UNITED STATES OF AMERICA

THE LONG SKELETON

I

THE SWEEP HAND of the electric wall clock trotted downstairs to "30" and began to trot up again. An assistant director held his right hand beyond his right ear, the index finger pointed stiffly upward. Amanda Towne looked at the tiny watch on her wrist with an expression of aggrieved surprise and shook her head at it, a lady betrayed by time. She turned—but not too far, with chin up—to the Grandmother of the Year, who sat beside her on the sofa, and shared with her, for two seconds by the count, the realization that the best of things must end.

The assistant director brought his finger down, as if it were a pistol and he a duelist. Amanda Towne turned to face front again, the camera shifted slightly, eliminating the Grandmother of the Year from further consideration.

"Isn't she just lovely?" Amanda Towne enquired, with a lilt—and just a touch of Arkansas—in her voice. "I know all of you out there wish she could just go on and on—and *on*. But—" She did not finish that; she moved graceful hands a little in resignation. She leaned forward slightly; her eyes were bright and her even teeth were brighter still on television screens from coast to coast. "Take care of yourselves, dear people," she said. "*Do* take care of yourselves. And now Jimmy has a word for you about our next guests and—" Again she did not finish, not in words. Her smile, for two seconds, lingered like a benediction.

Her face, and the smile with it, vanished from the monitor. It was replaced by the fatherly face of James Fergus, who said, "Thank *you*, Amanda Towne. And now, before I tell you about Friday's People Next Door, a word about Fluff, the deep penetrating—"

The camera was off Amanda Towne, the micro[illegible]which had dangled above her head—and the head of the G[illegible]other of the Year—climbed up its cable. "I—" the Grandmother of the

Year began, and Amanda put a finger to her lips. "—until Friday at the same time," the monitor said, in a soft deep voice, "when once more we will get together with the People Next Door in this great land of ours, goodbye and good luck from Amanda Towne and all of us. This is James Fergus speaking."

Amanda Towne took the finger from her lips; the smile came away with it.

"You were fine, Mrs. Burney," she said. "Just fine."

"I thought—" the Grandmother of the Year said.

"Just fine," Miss Amanda Towne said firmly. "I'm sure they all loved you." She stood up. "My God, Jimmy," she said. "Do you have to make it sound so damn much like a funeral? Can't you get just a little—" She did not finish this, either. She shrugged. "I suppose not," she said. "I suppose you just can't, can you?"

She turned away from James Fergus, who flushed a little, flushed slowly, and whose round face sagged a little.

"I—" the Grandmother of the Year said, "just want to—"

"You were fine," Amanda told her, and for an instant a smile came back—a trickle of a smile. "We all so much appreciated—oh, there you are."

She spoke over Mrs. Burney, whose sixteen grandchildren were doing so well, in so many places. She spoke to a short, heavy woman with sharp black eyes, with hair blacker than her eyes.

"Well?" Amanda Towne said.

The black-haired woman nodded briefly. She made, with thumb and middle finger of her right hand, an approving circle. She advanced on Mrs. Burney, who was slight and gray. She said, "Wonderful, my dear. Let me help you find your things," and seemed to engulf the Grandmother of the Year as she led her off.

"Whew!" Amanda Towne said and looked around the studio, now with no smile at all. She said, "Tony! Tony Gray!"

"Ye[illegible]*'am,*" Tony Gray said, and appeared from behind a camer[illegible]was wiry; he had red hair. He wore an expression of somewhat intense innocence.

"Well?" Amanda said, without sympathy. He started to speak, but was not permitted. "Don't try it," Amanda told him. "You talked to her. Well?"

"All right," Tony Gray said. "She froze a little, maybe."

" 'Yes, Miss Towne,' " Amanda said. " 'No, Miss Towne.' 'I guess that's right, Miss Towne.' 'I really couldn't say about that, Miss Towne.' "

"Now Mandy," Tony Gray said. "She froze. Every now and then it's bound to happen. Some of 'em do. Some don't. Chipper's a sparrow when I talked to her."

"She should have been a sparrow," Amanda Towne told him. "I'd rather interview a sparrow. With a flock of sparrow grandchildren."

"It wasn't that bad," Gray said. "She's a sweet old thing. That came over. Relax, Mandy. Some of 'em will always freeze. Even on People Next Door. I—"

"All tucked away in a cab," the black-haired woman said, from half across the studio. "Now don't get all worked up, Mandy."

"You heard it," Amanda Towne said. "Watched me prying words out with a crowbar. Smiling until my damned teeth ached. And Tony says some of them will always freeze. And you say don't get worked up. And—"

"There," Alice Fleming said. "There ducky."

She and Tony Gray looked at each other, briefly.

"Humor her," Amanda Towne said. "Smooth her down. Butter her up."

"Mandy," Alice Fleming said, "so maybe the last ten minutes was a little sticky. The rest was like silk. You tell her, Tony."

"Like silk," Tony Gray said. "In the groove, precisely." He grinned at Amanda. "Trouble is," he said, "you want to turn up an Honorable Parkman every day. Editorial in the *Times* today."

"With credit?"

"Well," Tony said, " 'a popular afternoon TV progr[illegible] 'a leading woman interviewer.' This was the *Times*, M[illegible] can't have everything."

Amanda Towne laughed, briefly, but her brief la[illegible]

Alice Fleming sighed, with the beginning of relaxation. Mandy was coming out of it; Mandy always came out of it, just as she always went into it. Well, if she didn't get keyed up, she wouldn't be Mandy—wouldn't be Amanda Towne, coast to coast and two stations in Canada; Amanda Towne, with more sponsors than you could shake a stick at (if sticks were ever shaken at sponsors) or work into an hour's show; Amanda Towne with a waiting list of ready-mixes, and things that cured and other things which penetrated deeply.

"He called me up," Amanda said. "Said, wasn't there anything I could do? I said, such as what Mr. Parkman? Innocent-like."

Arkansas returned, a little, to her voice, as it did when she was coming out of it, and remembering she was Amanda Towne, coast to coast, with a waiting list, neighbor to all next doors and folksy as they came.

"He seemed," Amanda Towne said, "to think I'd led him on. Imagine that."

They imagined it. Alice Fleming, business manager of Amanda Towne imagined it; Tony Gray, pre-broadcast interviewer for Amanda Towne, legman for Amanda Towne, imagined it. The three of them laughed happily.

"What a notion!" Tony said. "As if you'd do a thing like that!"

"That," Amanda said, "is what I told him. Innocent little me."

This was even funnier; they laughed contentedly at this.

"All the same," Tony Gray said, "he's out of business."

Amanda looked reflectively at a sign which said, "Positively No Smoking," and lighted a cigarette. She dragged at it deeply. Mrs. Alice Fleming sighed again, in further relief. Amanda was continuing to unwind.

"To be perfectly honest," Amanda said, and at that Tony Gray did not quite raise his reddish eyebrows, "I was innocent, in a mild way. I wanted to let a little stuffing out, but—" She moved [illegible]ers slightly under the beautifully fitting jacket of her [illegible]after all, all he said was—"

[illegible]nnotation, ducky," Mrs. Fleming said. "You and he together against a vulgar world. And don't tell me you didn't give him that idea. Don't tell *me!*"

"The little finger," Tony said, quickly, and was smiled at for his trouble. "The famous little finger of Amanda Towne, celebrated—"

"All right," Amanda said. "You've done your bits. Both of you. But just the same, Tony, one more—"

She did not finish that, or need to. Tony waited briefly, although he did not expect her to finish—or want her to finish.

"About the other thing?" he said. "The one you clam up about?"

"We'll see," Amanda said. "That is, I'll see."

She nodded, agreeing with herself.

"And," she said, "no innocence this time. Well?"

"Yes, ducky," Mrs. Alice Fleming said. "You want to sit in with Bart and me?"

And wished she hadn't, because Amanda Towne's blue eyes narrowed a little, and iced a little.

"That," she said, "is something you ought to be able to handle, darling." She paused. "That—anyway," she said. "Considering—" She paused longer. "Everything," she said, and put a fur stole around her shoulders. And went.

Tony Gray and Alice Fleming watched her go.

"Chip on her shoulder today," Tony said. "Nice mink chip." He lighted a cigarette of his own. "Of course," he said, "it takes all kinds to make a meal-ticket, I always say."

"I wouldn't," Alice Fleming told him, "always say it out loud, sonny."

***

"*Do* take care of yourselves," the clear and friendly voice pleaded from the television set and Pamela North, thus admonished, took the most immediate step, which seemed to [illegible] a knob. As the knob turned the whitest of smiles [illegible] until it was only the brightness of perfect teeth. Like [illegible] ire Cat, Pam North thought, and then there was [illegible] dot in the center of the screen—a dot so hotly white that one would have thought it could burn through glass. It never had, Pam told herself, and thought, So that's Amanda Towne, and all you have to do, really, to have grandchildren is to make a start and wait to see what happens, although that doesn't, certainly, ensure that one grandchild will be a judge and another president of a college. (Even a small college.) The poor thing was scared stiff, Pam North thought, and I hope Mr. Prentori isn't going to be late.

Mr. Prentori was not; Mr. Prentori came most carefully on his hour, which was three o'clock of the afternoon of Wednesday, November thirteenth. The doorbell rang twice, shortly, and Martini, last of her tribe (who had been comfortable on a chair, watching Amanda Towne with a hard blue gaze), vanished, more rapidly than any Cheshire Cat. Thinks it's the vet again, poor baby, Pam thought, and went to the door, where Mr. Prentori waited with buckets. "You're right on time," Pam said, keeping the astonishment out of her voice, and Mr. Prentori said, "Sure, why not?", to which there was no answer. (Except that painters never are, which would have been unkind.)

Mr. Prentori came into the living room of the apartment and regarded it. "Flattener streaked through last time, didn't it?" Mr. Prentori said, rather darkly. "You want the same color, I guess?" With this, a kind of eager cheerfulness invaded his voice.

"No," Pam said. "I'm afraid not, Mr. Prentori."

"Oh," Mr. Prentori said. He sighed, rather ostentatiously. He said, "Well." He said, "The whole apartment, the man said. Same colors in the other rooms?"

"No," Pam said. "I'm afraid not, Mr. Prentori." Mr. Prentori, boss painter, had large brown eyes. Sadness dripped from them.

"Everything different?" he said, hoping against hope.

"I'm afraid so," Pam said.

"You've got ideas what you want?"

[illegible]ard to break it to Mr. Prentori. Pam steeled herself.

[illegible] "Yes," and the word hung in the room, like the last [illegible] a dirge of bells.

"In here," Pam said, "we thought—a kind of warm gray? With just a touch of something? Green? But not a green green, if you know what I mean?"

"No," Mr. Prentori said. "How would I know what you mean, Mrs. North? A warm *green?*"

It was, Pam thought, going to be as it always was, as every two years it was. This would be one for that Amanda Towne, full of helpful hints for housewives, knowing easier ways to do almost everything. One had only to look at Amanda Towne, bright and clear on television, mistress of everything, to know that boss painters would be malleable in her expert hands. Malleable as, for example, putty, which seemed appropriate.

"Have to put on a sizing coat," Mr. Prentori said. "Streaked the way it is with flattener. Green isn't a warm color, Mrs. North." He looked around the room again. "Your husband do this himself last time?" he asked, his voice as lacking in warmth as the color green.

"My husband," Pam said, "can't stand the smell of paint. It makes him sick."

"Makes me sick too," Mr. Prentori said. "But there you are."

It was not clear to Pamela North quite where they were. Painters, Pam thought, do slip through your fingers somehow. Because there are no words for colors, as there are no words for the sound of music, a kind of evasiveness, deriving from the medium, pervades the character; because—

"Well," Mr. Prentori said, "we may as well try. Start with gray and see." He spread a paint-spattered canvas. He grouped buckets and cans. He said, "Personally, I'd say an off-white. Room's sort of dark and—"

"Gray," Pam North said. "A soft gray, with a little green, but as warm as—"

"Too much like butter—" Pam said, much later, in another room. "No, not so pink. Hardly pink at all," she said, some time after that. "A little more something," she said, at a quarter after four in the last room, slightly ill from the smell of paint, colors swimming meaninglessly behind her eyes—green only another gray, pink (but not *really* pink) hardly to be told from magenta; all decisiveness lost and all assurance and, in some mysterious fashion achieved, a spot of paint (pink? warm gray?) on the very tip of her nose.

It was so, collapsed in a chair, Martini on her lap, that Jerry found her at five, home early from the office. Jerry opened the door and put his head in and said, "Oh-my-God-no!" and pulled his head out again, and breathed deeply of the corridor air (not in itself anything to send blood coursing through veins) and went in, holding his breath as long as he could. Martini left Pam's lap to greet, aggrievedly, with protest in a penetrating Siamese voice. Pam continued to stare at a wall streaked with paint in slightly different intensities. She said, "Hello, Jerry," in a small and distant voice. He leaned over the chair and kissed her. "You taste of paint," he said.

"Everything does," Pam said.

"I'd forgotten," Jerry said. "I know you told me, but—Freud, I suppose."

"It was time," Pam said, disconsolately. "It's been two years. Mr. Prentori said the streaks are flattener, whatever that is. He says maybe by Saturday night, except that will mean overtime and it's up to the man, whoever he is, so probably it won't be until Monday. And I can't tell one color from another any more. Do you want—?"

"No," Jerry said. "Whatever you've decided. When?"

"Eight o'clock tomorrow morning," Pam said. "Of course we could—the way we did last time—only it means—because Martini's the only one now and all by herself—and anyway—do you think we ought to?"

It is sometimes contended, by the inexperienced, that Pamela North is not always lucid in speech; she has even, by some, been accused of ellipsis.

"Have you tried?" Jerry asked her. She nodded.

"Most of them don't like cats," she said. "The Breckenridge says, only if it's a suite, and we're responsible for chairs and things."

“How much?” Jerry said.

“Well,” Pam said, “thirty-five, actually.”

Gerald North said, “Ouch.”

“Paint makes her sick, too,” Pam said. “And that means the vet.”

Jerry shuddered slightly.

“Of course,” Pam said, “nobody ever said we had to have a cat.”

Martini said something like “Oo-wow-oo!” on a protracted note, dismissing this nonsense.

“Martha doesn't mind coming down early to let them in,” Pam said. “And it might be only until late Saturday and—”

“Pam,” Jerry said, “did you reserve?”

“Well,” Pam said, “it's you the paint makes sick mostly, and they want to start in the bedroom and everything will taste of it, including cocktails, but of course—” She stopped, being looked at. “Yes,” Pam said.

“And pack?”

“Well—”

***

“Stately” is perhaps the word for the Hotel Breckenridge, just off Fifth in Manhattan's Fifties, although the term “spacious” also is employed, particularly by the management. The lobbies are extensive, and dignity prevails, and the restaurant most frequented is wood paneled, with small, red-shaded, lamps on tables. It is not always possible to see precisely what one is eating, but the flavors are gratifying. Spaciousness extends to the upper floors; the suite provided the Norths, complete with the cat named Martini, who spoke harshly through the grating of the traveling box she detests, would have been more than ample for a much larger family. Even Martini, who is assiduous, tired after she had smelled only the living room, left bedroom and bath for the future, and curled under a chair—under it, just in case, having lived a dozen years by taking thought in such matters. In strange places, a cat never knows.

The living room was long, with windows at the end which opened on a court. The living room was also extravagantly wide; the bedroom was only a little smaller, and the two beds were double beds. The bathroom, which opened from the entrance hall, had a tub in which Jerry could—if he chose, as he did not, being a man for showers—lie full length, and in which Pam could, briefly at any rate, have swum. In two words, Pam summarized the amplitude of the Hotel Breckenridge. "My goodness!" Pam said, with conviction.

It was six when they checked in—the reservation ready, a cat (providing compensation was guaranteed for clawed fabrics or other nuisances) acceptable. It was a little after seven when they went out to dinner, bathed and fortified by martinis, those also spacious, brought to the room.

It was a quarter of eleven when they returned, having dined pleasantly, although not in the paneled restaurant of the Breckenridge—"It makes me feel like the last century," Pam explained and added, after a moment's thought, and to clarify, "any last century." They had seen the latter two-thirds of a movie, those being, Pam feels, the two-thirds most worth seeing, since during them, if ever, things happen.

Lights burned softly in the living room when they went into it and, when called, Martini came out from under a sofa, stretched and commented briefly, but with profanity—with profanity of a certain kind. "Oh dear!" Pam North said, "we *couldn't* have!" and turned back to look toward the bathroom. "Damn!" Pam said, and walked to the bathroom and opened the closed door. "Yah!" Martini said, with bitterness, and went into the bathroom, her rear end wagging indignation. The sound of a cat scratching torn newspaper emerged from the bathroom; the sound was violent, being occasioned by a cat whose patience had been tried almost—the Norths hoped not quite—to the breaking point.

"Which of us?" Pam said, and Jerry shook his head, and thought neither, which was momentarily mysterious. He had—

he was very sure he had—checked on the bathroom door as they went out, made sure it was open for Martini's needs.

"Of course," Pam said, "she could have closed it herself, I suppose, although it's hard to see why, and if she did, she'd be inside. Unless—" She did not finish, but walked quickly toward the bedroom. "That's it," she said, speaking into the bedroom from the doorway. "The maid to turn down the—" And she stopped there—stopped so suddenly, so much as if her breath had been cut off, that Jerry, reaching for the door of the hall closet, whirled, still holding his topcoat.

Pam did not call out, and did not scream. But her slim right hand clung to the doorframe as if, without support, she would have fallen. Jerry was behind her, his topcoat dropped to the floor and forgotten there, and held her shoulders and looked over her head into the bedroom—looked at what she saw, at what had caught the breath from her.

A woman Jerry had never seen before lay on the bed most distant from the door. She was dressed in a gray suit, the jacket neatly buttoned. She lay on her back, her head on one of the pillows of the turned-down bed. She might have lain down to rest and fallen gently asleep, and Jerry, looking into the softly lighted room, almost spoke the word which would—which surely would—awaken her. But he knew before he spoke that she would not hear the word. Her eyes were open, so she did not sleep; she lay, now looked at more carefully, with a curious stiffness. And the clearly modeled face had a peculiar blueness of the skin.

Seeing so much, Jerry did not need to go farther into the room, but he went into the room, and stood looking down at the dead woman. He touched her face gently, and found it without warmth, as he had known he would, and rigid under his fingers. He looked away from her, and toward Pam—her hand still clenching the doorframe; the knuckles white with the intensity of the pressure. He did not need to say anything. He walked to her and said, meaninglessly, "All right, Pam," although things were certainly not all right. She looked up at him, and her expression was a question.

"I don't know," Jerry said. "It looks—it looks as though she had just lain down and died. Some time ago, I think. Rigor's—" He did not finish. "I never saw her before," he said. "I—"

But Pam said, "Wait," and went into the bedroom and stood for a moment looking down at the woman who lay so peacefully dead. She faced Jerry again, and now, slowly, with a kind of carefulness, she nodded her head.

"On television," Pam said, and spoke as slowly, as carefully, as she had moved her head. "She interviewed people. This afternoon—" She shook her head, then. "It doesn't matter," she said. "I watched while—" She paused again, and Jerry waited.

"I can't think of her name," Pam said. "It's—wait a minute. Towne. Something—Amanda Towne, that's it. Amanda Towne."

She walked back to Jerry, then, and they went into the living room, Jerry's arm about her shoulders. "I'm all right," Pam said, and clearly was not, and sat a moment on a sofa. "I'm all right," she said again, after a few moments, and Jerry, watching her, saw a deep breath lift in her chest and said, "Sure you are," which by then was true.

"Only," Pam said, in much her normal voice, "it's such a dreadful thing. She looks so—so alive. And this afternoon she—"

"All right," Jerry said, and moved toward the telephone.

"Such a—such an awful color," Pam said. "Her face so—"

"Yes," Jerry said. "A very peculiar color. We'll have—" He took the telephone from its cradle, and it was silent at his ear. Pointlessly, he moved it a little from his ear and shook it, and then, as if in answer, a clear voice spoke in his ear—spoke with careful sweetness, the utmost of attention.

"Your order, please?" the girl somewhere said.

Jerry North hesitated, momentarily. Absurdly, he was tempted to say, in a tone to match her tone, "Would you mind sending up for a body?" He said, "Will you call the police, please?" and waited.

"Thank you," the girl said, in precisely the same politely attentive voice. "I'll—*what? What did you say?*"

The mind works slowly; momentum briefly guards the mind from the unexpected, the unbelievable.

"The police," Jerry said, and was patient. "I'm afraid there is—" It was somehow difficult to put it bluntly. It was a thing to be broken gently. "I'm afraid there's been an—an accident," he said, which he did not suppose to be true, or to be especially gentle. "That is, a woman seems to have—died. In our room. The room is—" For a moment he could not remember. He read the typed notation in the base of the telephone. "Seven-eighteen," he said. "My wife—"

"*Dead?*" the switchboard girl said. The veneer had cracked off her voice. "You say somebody's *dead?*"

Jerry did. He said it again.

"*Oh-my-God!*" the girl said, as one word. "Who?"

It was to the point, of course; unexpectedly to the point.

"My wife," Jerry said, "thinks it may be a Miss Towne. She does something on—"

"*Towne!*" the girl said. "*Oh-my-God-not-Miss Towne!*"

"I'm afraid—" Jerry said.

"But," the girl said, "she *lives* here. Here in the hotel. I don't—"

"No," Jerry said, "I don't either. But you'd better call the police."

II

THE POLICE CAME. A hotel detective came first, and a Mr. Mimms, who was an assistant manager, and dressed for it, and who mopped his forehead with a monogramed handkerchief—and agreed, horror in his voice, that the dead woman was indeed Amanda Towne, and asked, several times, "How did she get here?" which nobody could answer, and, also several times, "Terrible. Simply *terrible*," with which nobody was inclined to disagree. But the police came; uniformed men first, and then men not in uniform; photographers came, and fingerprint men. Amanda Towne, who had faced many cameras, with an expression for each of them, had no expression whatever now for these cameras which peered down at her, and functioned in the hardest, the least sympathetic, of light. An assistant medical examiner came and, when the pictures had been taken, examined the body briefly and looked at the precinct lieutenant and shrugged.

"Well?" the precinct man said. "So what, doctor?"

"Dead several hours," the doctor said. "Four. Five maybe."

"Of what?"

The assistant medical examiner shrugged again, with greater emphasis. He spread his hands as he shrugged.

"Well," he said. "She wasn't shot. Wasn't stabbed. Wasn't hit over the head. Wasn't strangled."

"Thanks," the precinct lieutenant said. "Ate something that disagreed with her?"

"Possibly," the assistant medical examiner said. "Or had a thrombosis. Or took poison. Or—damned near anything. We'll find out."

"Guess," the precinct lieutenant said. "We won't hold it against you, doctor."

The doctor looked again, looked carefully, at the bluishly livid face; at the lips which had smiled so few hours before. He bent very close to the dead, stiffening face. He looked up.

"All right," he said, "an autopsy will tell. Nothing else. It's one of the most difficult things to spot, but—" He paused. The precinct lieutenant was patient, rather elaborately patient. "Asphyxia," the doctor said. "At a guess—just at a guess. I'd say she could have been smothered. With something that didn't bruise." He looked at the bed. "Like a pillow," he said.

There were two pillows on the wide bed, on one of which Amanda Towne's head rested. They moved the body, then, and both pillows were spotless white, one indented where the head had been. The precinct lieutenant tilted the lamp between the beds, and turned the pillows over. On the underside of the pillow Amanda Towne's head had rested on there was, faint but clear enough, a smear of red.

"Lipstick," the precinct lieutenant said, as if that were obvious, as if that were already proved. But nobody argued with him.

The Norths had sat side by side on a sofa in the living room, and a uniformed man had stood in the hallway leading to the door of the suite and looked at them. His expression was dispassionate, not really inimical. Detectives passing in and out—there is much going in and out at such times, all of it ordered, not all of it self-explanatory—looked at the Norths in passing, with judgment reserved, and curiosity only professional. Looked at detachedly, Jerry North thought, we're in something of a spot, with a good deal to explain and no explanations handy. But of course— As soon as Bill gets here, Pam thought, more immediately to the point. If it is murder, of course. She considered that. As I suppose it will be, because it always seems to be and—

It was, they both thought, about time for Bill—for Captain William Weigand, Homicide, Manhattan West, who would know (whatever it looked like) that this was only one more of those things which happened to the Norths, lightning rods for homicide—to show up, to take over. They would sit then no more in Coventry, judgment would no longer be so obviously reserved.

The uniformed man near the door heard something and turned to open the door. Three men came through it, and Sergeant Stein was the first. "Here they are now," Pam said, softly, not without relief. Another man came through the door. He was not anybody the Norths knew. A third man came—a large man, red of face, a man choleric with authority.

Jerry North could feel his eyes widening, looked at Pam, who looked quickly at him, and saw her eyes wide too. Then they both looked at Deputy Chief Inspector Artemus O'Malley, Commanding Detectives, Borough of Manhattan.

And Inspector O'Malley looked at them—looked with rising color. Across the room, Inspector Artemus O'Malley bristled at Pam and Jerry North.

It seemed, for a moment, as if Inspector O'Malley might explode. It was unfortunate that, just then, the cat Martini chose to come out from under the sofa, to see what there was for a cat to see.

O'Malley made a great sound—a sound without words, which was rather like a roar. Martini crouched and hissed, turned, and was a *café-au-lait* streak to the safety of cave the sofa made. She growled a penetrating Siamese growl.

O'Malley steadied himself, but his color did not lessen. It was clear he sought control.

"*My God!*" O'Malley said, and his voice filled the room, made the big room shrink, made it shudder. "*You two!*" He paused to gain control. "*And a cat!*" Inspector O'Malley said. But now he screamed. And from beneath the sofa, Martini, who had had enough of all of it, screamed back.

"She hates to be yelled at," Pam North said, without emphasis, by way of explanation. "All loud noises."

O'Malley swelled further, which could hardly, Pam thought, be good for him.

"Who's a loud noise?" Inspector O'Malley shouted, and advanced a step, and Jerry North found himself rising carefully from the sofa. The suite had, until then, been filled with little noises—the sounds of people moving, of men talking quietly.

Now, momentarily, there was no sound in the two rooms; it was as if Deputy Chief Inspector O'Malley's roaring voice had blown all lesser sounds away. Everything listened.

"It's only," Pam said, "that cats have very sensitive ears. Because they spread out so, inspector." She looked up at him. "Like funnels," she said. "On pivots, of course."

Inspector O'Malley drew in a massive breath. He exhaled it, seemingly molecule by molecule. His lips parted and were rejoined. And he turned, abruptly, on Detective Sergeant Stein, on the other detective who had entered with him.

"Well," O'Malley said, "waiting for a streetcar?"

And he turned away and led, massively, toward the bedroom. The nameless detective followed at his heels. Stein, for an instant, hesitated. There was half a smile on his dark, sensitive face. His eyebrows went up slightly. "On another case," he said. "Out of town." And then, quickly, he went after Inspector O'Malley who, all too evidently, had taken matters into his own hard hands.

It was clear enough—it was much too clear—what Stein had been talking about. He had been talking about Captain William Weigand, on another case and out of town on it. With Mullins, evidently, which didn't help at all.

"Even the inspector," Pam said, her voice low, "can't think we—I mean, merely because she came in here to—to die. Or—they must think to get killed. Because—"

She stopped. Jerry was moving his head slowly from side to side.

"Why not?" Jerry said.

Pam blinked her eyes quickly.

"Because—" she said, and then stopped. Jerry waited. After a time, a little heavily, he said, "Precisely." The uniformed man had moved out of the hall and closer to them. He listened.

"It's chilly in here, isn't it?" Pam North said. Jerry took her nearest hand. And they waited. Sounds came from the bedroom, with O'Malley's rumbling voice as an obbligato. After a time, men began to come from the bedroom—the photographers came, the medical examiner came, some of the precinct men came. But nobody said anything to Pam and Jerry North, although all looked at them. After what seemed a very long time, two men came in with a rolled stretcher and, after a short time, went out with it, no longer rolled, no longer empty. And then, finally, O'Malley came out, with Stein and the other homicide man following him. O'Malley stopped in front of the Norths.

He was no longer especially choleric; his gray eyes, however, did nothing to raise the temperature.

"All right," he said. "Let's have your story." He pulled a straight-backed chair forward and sat in it—a massive man, filled with massive disbelief. "Take it down, Williams," he said, without looking at Williams, and the man who had come in with the inspector and Stein found chair and table, and stenographer's notebook.

"Well," Pam said, "it's only that Mr. Prentori was coming to paint and paint makes Jerry sick and everything tastes of it. So we—"

"All right, Pam," Jerry said, quickly, because it appeared to him that O'Malley had begun to swell.

"But," Pam said, "Bill likes to have everything because who knows what may turn out to be—you're hurting my hand, Jerry."

"Sorry," Jerry said, and lessened his grip. "Listen, Inspector O'Malley—we came here to spend a couple of nights because our apartment's being painted. We checked in and—"

"One thing at a time," O'Malley said. "You looked in the bedroom? I suppose you say she wasn't there?"

"Nobody was there," Jerry said.

"The boy turned on all the lights," Pam said. "We couldn't have missed—"

"All right," O'Malley said. "All right. You knew her, though. Told the people downstairs it was Miss Towne. You want to say you didn't know her?"

"On TV was all," Pam said. "Actually, I don't think I ever saw her until this afternoon. I couldn't start anything because

Mr. Prentori was coming so soon and so I just—it was about the Grandmother of the Year. You can ask anybody."

"The Grandmother—" O'Malley began and caught himself, with obvious effort. "You," he said, and pointed at Jerry North, "suppose you just tell what you say happened. You checked in—"

"Changed," Jerry said. "I'd just come from the office."

"Yeah," O'Malley said. "You publish books." He said it darkly; obscurely, it became an accusation. "So then what?"

They had gone out. Jerry thought a little after seven. They had had dinner.

"Here?"

It had not been there. It had been—

"Left your key at the desk, I suppose," O'Malley said, in the tone of one who supposes nothing of the kind.

"No," Jerry said. "Who does?"

"Don't waste so damn much time," O'Malley said. "I'm not Weigand. Just tell me what happened. What you say happened. You went out and had dinner. Where?"

"Well," Pam said, "we started for the Algonquin, of course. But we saw this movie—I mean I remembered about the movie—anyway—we decided to have a quick dinner, because at the Algonquin it always takes us a long time, what with one thing and another and it's such a pleasant place to talk, you know and—you're hurting my hand again, Jerry."

It was, Jerry thought, better her hand than her neck which, from O'Malley's expression, seemed to be in some peril. But, again, he relaxed pressure.

"The Brass Rail," he said. "We both had roast beef and—"

"For God's sake," O'Malley said. "What's roast beef got to do with it? Just don't clutter it up so damn much."

They knew of Inspector O'Malley's idiosyncrasies more from Bill Weigand, who worked under him, as did all Manhattan's detectives, than from previous direct association. Cases in which the Norths were involved were, in O'Malley's mind, cases to be avoided—they were, as Mullins also put it, "screwy" cases. ("The inspector likes things simple," Bill had told them. "Not that he isn't a damn good cop. It's just that—" Bill had paused, seeking a word. "He doesn't like things cluttered up," Bill had said, and grinned at them, and said that they couldn't deny they tended to clutter things up. "Not when they aren't cluttered already," Pam had said, with some indignation.)

"You asked where," Jerry said. "The Brass Rail. Nobody knows us there so—"

"And," O'Malley said, "you didn't leave your key at the desk, like you're supposed to. Anybody see you go out? Out of here?"

"Dozens, probably," Jerry said.

"Anybody you know. Anybody can say, 'Sure, I saw Mr. and Mrs. North go out of the Breckenridge at twelve minutes after seven, on the nose, and get a cab and—' "

"No," Jerry said. "And we didn't get a cab. We walked."

It could not be said that O'Malley snorted. It could not, on the other hand, be said with confidence that he did not snort.

"All right," O'Malley said, "what you say is you left here a little after seven, and went to dinner at the Brass Rail, although this hotel is full of restaurants—pretty good restaurants from what I hear—and didn't take a cab, so nobody can check that out, and—who'd you see knows you at the Brass Rail?"

"Nobody," Jerry said. "Listen, inspector, people do things all the time they can't prove—"

"Skip it," O'Malley said. "You ate this roast beef. So—"

They had gone to a movie. In spite of the earlier dinner, the rather less leisurely atmosphere, they had been late for the movie —gone in, found seats, when the film was, at a guess, about a third run. They named the movie.

"Kept your seat stubs, probably?" O'Malley said.

They had not. Who did?

"H-mmm," O'Malley said, with meaning. "You got in late, you say. What time did you get back here?"

"About a quarter of eleven."

"Get a cab back?"

They had not.

"H-mmm," O'Malley said. "Stayed over to see the first part of this movie, probably?"

They had not.

"Because," Pam said, "that spoils them sometimes, don't you think? I mean, if you go in in the middle, they seem—I mean most movies seem—so much better than they are. More—subtle? But if you stay through—and there are almost always cartoons, anyway, and usually the ones where they do dreadful things to a cat—the—where was I?"

"God knows," O'Malley said. "If you'll—"

"Oh yes," Pam said, "if you stay through, it all makes just ordinary sense and you haven't anything to ponder about. Like in this one—if she felt that way about him, why did she marry him in the first place? They put the explanations first, usually."

"Look," O'Malley said, "how can they put the explanation in before there's anything to—" He stopped abruptly. "That's enough of that," he said, with an almost violent firmness—a firmness, Jerry suspected, directed inward, toward the inner O'Malley. "You came in here," he said, "and found Miss Towne, a woman you'd never met before, on your bed." He said this to Mr. North, a little carefully, even a little anxiously, he did not look at Pam.

"Jerry's or mine," Pam said. "We hadn't decided yet. Does it matter a great deal, inspector?"

"It—" O'Malley said, loudly, and caught himself. "On one of the beds," he said.

Jerry nodded.

"Perfectly strange woman," O'Malley said, "comes into your hotel room while you're out going to a movie and gets herself killed. Why? How'd she get in? I suppose you're going to say the door was open?"

"No," Jerry said, "the door was locked. She must have had a key. Somebody must have had a key."

"Two duplicates," O'Malley said. "Both in the mailbox where they belong. *You* had a key."

"Yes."

"She *was* killed, then?" Pam said.

"I'll ask the questions," O'Malley said. "Just let me ask the questions, huh? Sure she was killed. That is—sure she was." He looked at them closely. "Given poison," he said.

They were supposed, Pam thought, to react to that; to say, or do, something which would reveal. There was open expectancy on O'Malley's florid face. They were supposed to look—relieved? surprised? Then it wasn't really—

"Look like you don't buy that, North," O'Malley said, and spoke quickly, spoke hard. Pam looked at her husband and thought, The poor dear. And thought, What an unconcealing face he has, really, because Jerry did not look at all as if he were buying that.

Jerry shrugged. He said he wasn't a doctor; he said if the medical examiner—

"You thought it was something else," O'Malley told him. "What?"

"From the color of her face," Jerry said, "I thought she might have died of asphyxiation. Perhaps—"

He paused.

"Well?" O'Malley said. "What?"

"—been smothered," Jerry said. "With a pillow, perhaps. There's a bluish lividity, usually, if it's asphyxiation and there weren't any marks to show—"

He stopped, having finally got it—got it from the look of contentment on O'Malley's florid face; a look almost of a cat who has found cream. (The poor dear, Pam thought of Jerry. Not that most of them really like cream, she thought, for no reason in particular.)

"Very interesting," O'Malley said. "I'll have to tell the M.E. that. Took his man a long time just to guess and here you come up with it. You must be a doctor, North. On the side."

North Books, Inc., had recently published an abridged toxicology. Jerry had skimmed through it, since Pam and he seemed, nowadays, so often to be in situations where some smattering of toxicology and medical jurisprudence might prove helpful. He had read about the bluish lividity. He had—

He stopped the explanation—stopped because O'Malley listened with interest so acted out, nodded so often to show he followed, looked so very much like a cat with cream.

"Sure," O'Malley said. "That explains that. Funny thing you and this Miss Towne hadn't run into each other. Before now."

They looked at him.

"Books," O'Malley said. "TV. Advertising. All that sort of thing. Same breed of—cats." He said "cats" with a certain emphasis; an emphasis, Pam thought, of loathing. ("In addition," Bill had said, when explaining O'Malley's antipathy to Norths in cases, "he's heard you have cats. He hates cats.")

It was unfortunate that Martini, hearing her race mentioned, responded, from underneath the sofa, with a Siamese remark. It was only an answer, really, on hearing cats referred to. But the Siamese voice is seldom dulcet. O'Malley glared at the sofa, with loathing.

"One thing we forgot," Pam said, thus reminded. "When we went out we left the bathroom door open, so Martini could—that is, go to it. We put her pan in there, you know. The pan with paper in it? And—"

"For God's sake," O'Malley said. "So what in God's name?"

"Only when we came back it was closed," Pam said. "We thought the maid—wait a minute. The maid was in here. Closed the door and turned down the beds and—"

She was told to wait a minute.

"Well," O'Malley said, and said it to Sergeant Stein, "where is she? This maid?"

It would, Pam thought, have been unfortunate for Sergeant Stein if he could not, immediately, have pulled a maid out of a hat. As it happened, he could. He did. O'Malley paid this foresight the tribute of a brief nod.

The maid was Rose Pinkney. She was thirty-seven years old and lived in Brooklyn, and was a widow, and none of these things mattered, except to her. She worked the evening shift at the Hotel Breckenridge; worked from six until midnight. She turned down beds. (That she and others should be employed to go in the evenings from room to room, knocking on doors of rooms listed as occupied, waiting, saying, "Sorry, the maid," if they were answered, going in if they were not and taking spreads from beds and folding them neatly, turning down covers and upper sheet at a certain angle, prescribed—that this went on nightly in the Hotel Breckenridge always slightly puzzled Rose Pinkney. Guests could, she supposed, learn to turn down their own beds or, more simply, merely get into them. If she were running a hotel— But she was not, of course, and the work was light and the hours no worse than most hours. Better than cleaning offices in the middle of the night.)

That the routine had come to this puzzled Rose Pinkney even more. News of what it had come to, spread through the housekeeper's department rapidly, and in many forms. A man had been murdered on the seventh floor, and there was blood all over everything. No, a couple on their honeymoon had shot one another. No—no—on the other hand—

And now she was in the middle of it, which was exciting, but made her ill at ease. She tugged at the skirt of her uniform, which needed no tugging at. The big, red-faced man said, "Miss Pinkney," and she said, "No, Missis Pinkney, please." He said, "All right," impatiently and she flushed slightly. But, firmly, she said, "Missis Pinkney it is, on account of—"

"All *right*," Inspector O'Malley said, rather more firmly. "You worked this floor tonight?"

"Corridor," she said. "Not the whole floor, mister. On account of—"

"Corridor," O'Malley said. But now he smiled at her. "Of course, Mrs. Pinkney," he said. "This room?"

She nodded. She looked at the others in the room—at the man in a gray suit taking notes; at the "dark-complected" man who wasn't doing anything she could see, but who had met her at the door of the suite and brought her in; at the man and woman sitting side by side on a sofa, close together. Probably the ones who had done it, Rose Pinkney thought. Whatever it was. Murder, from what they said.

"To turn down the beds," she said. "Like every night. If somebody's rented the room, that is to say."

O'Malley could be patient, particularly with those who made sense—ordinary, everyday simple sense. (Didn't talk about movies being better if—) He was patient with Rose Pinkney.

She had knocked at the door of Suite 718 at a quarter after seven, or thereabouts. Being unanswered, she had gone in and done what she was supposed to do. She described it.

"Show us," O'Malley told her, and was still patient—she was to pretend she was coming in the door to the suite, was to do over what she had done earlier. When she got the idea, Rose said, "Okay," and went out into the outer corridor and closed the door after her and then knocked on it. Stein went and let her in. She said, "Only nobody's supposed to be here. If they are, I'm supposed to come back later," and Stein said, he knew, and that she was to pretend they weren't there.

She shook her head (thinking it pretty silly) and came into the suite. She went first into the bathroom, and came out of it and closed the door. "See if they need fresh towels," she said. "If the wastebasket's full."

"Sure," O'Malley said. "Nobody in the bathroom the first time?"

"*Mister,*" she said, "like I told you, we make sure nobody's in the room."

"You always close the bathroom door?" O'Malley asked, and she said, "I guess so," and thought, and said, "Sure, I guess so." She was told to go on. She went across the living room. She looked into a wastebasket and went into the bedroom. She came back. "Turned down already," she said. "Want I should make them up and *then* turn them down?"

"No," O'Malley said. "That's all you do? You did it this way earlier?"

"Nobody let me in," she said, "on account of, there was nobody here. Like I told you. I used my pass key."

"When you come in," Mrs. North said, "do you leave the door open? The door to the corridor?"

Rose looked at Mrs. North. She looked at the inspector, who said he'd ask the questions, if it was all right with everybody and then, "All right, do you?"

She did, she always did. So people would know she was in there. In case they didn't notice the cart.

"All right," O'Malley said. "The cart? What's the cart?"

People didn't know very much, and that was a fact. (But she did not say so.) The cart was on wheels; it had a rack for fresh towels; a bin for soiled towels; a receptacle for the contents of overflowing wastebaskets. It was left outside a room being worked in. "Nobody said to bring the cart," Rose said.

"That's all right," O'Malley said. "Just getting the picture. And there wasn't anybody in here when you came in?"

"Nobody I saw."

"Not even," Pam said, "a cat?"

"I'll—" O'Malley said. "Well, you didn't see a cat, Mrs. Pinkney? Funny-looking cat?"

He looked at Mrs. North quickly, with a fleeting expression of pleasure.

"She looks like any—" Pam said, rising to the bait, and had her hand pressed. "Anyway, she'd go under something until she found out who it was, because she'd know it wasn't us."

"Did you," O'Malley said, "see anything of a cat, Mrs. Pinkney? Or hear anything?"

"No." But then she said, "Only there was this pan in the bathroom, with torn paper in it. So I figured—your cat, miss?"

"Yes," Pam said. "A Siamese cat. Not funny-looking at all, really."

"Mine's red," Rose said. "Always have a red cat. Feed yours liver?"

"No," Pam said. "It's not really good for them. As a regular diet, I mean. And if you give them some now and then, they get so they won't eat anything else. But Martini doesn't like it anyway and—"

"Won't eat nothing else, mine won't," Rose said. "Liver or nothing, that's the old redhead. 'Cept fish, of course. Likes a piece of fish as well as the next—"

"All *right*," O'Malley said, swelling ominously, Jerry thought. "*All right!*"

"You mean," Mrs. Pinkney said, "you don't want me any more?"

"That's right," O'Malley said. "Go—go home and feed your damned cat." This hurt her feelings. Her face showed it. "Sorry if I—" she began, and O'Malley made the effort.

"You did fine, Mrs. Pinkney," he said. "Didn't mean to yell at you."

"Well!" she said, and started out. Stein went with her. Stein came back.

"You see," Pam North said, "how Miss Towne could have got in. Or anybody. Or Miss Towne *and* anybody. While the maid was in the bedroom before she left and—"

"Listen," O'Malley said and there was, Jerry thought, an unexpected note in the inspector's voice—a note almost of entreaty. "Listen, Mrs. North, suppose you let me do it, huh?"

"Of course, inspector," Pam said. "I was just trying—"

"Just don't, please," the inspector said. "That's all I ask, lady."

III

IT HAD NOT BEEN, of course. Inspector Artemus O'Malley had asked a great deal more, and asked much of it over and over, and asked much of it with evident doubt that he was being truthfully answered. But finally, at a little after two o'clock in the morning, he had said that that was all for now and that they could go. This, for a few moments, presented something of a problem. They could not, of course, sleep what remained of the night in Suite 718. They could get another room in the hotel—perhaps. "Let's go home," Pam said. "I don't like hotel life as much as I thought I would. We can do something about Mr. Prentori."

They packed up again—packed their clothes, got Martini from under the sofa and packed her (and she was furious) and got a cab, after some waiting, and went home. "It's not the same without Bill," Pam said, moodily. "Bill would know that we didn't have anything to—" Jerry waited, and heard nothing more, except soft and steady breathing. Some time later, he went to sleep himself.

Almost instantly, bells rang and buckets banged and while the Norths struggled out of sleep, there was heavy knocking at the apartment door. "They've come for us," Pam said. "Oh my goodness." But "they" had not. Mr. Prentori had come, with aides, with buckets, with stepladders. He had come early; it was only seven-thirty when he came. The Norths fled—they fed Martini and put her in the kitchen, and left a note for Martha, and fled. They paused in flight at a near-by Schrafft's, and had accumulated newspapers by then. The newspapers were full of the death of Amanda Towne. There was in them also a good deal about Mr. and Mrs. North—Gerald North, head of North Books, Inc., and his "attractive wife." The *Herald Tribune* reminded its readers that the Norths had been, before, involved in crimes of violence. The *Herald Tribune* had the discretion to add "innocently" but—rather unkindly, Pam thought—qualified with, "in the past."

"All we're going to find out this time is what we read in the newspapers," Pam said, and read in the *Herald Tribune*. And Jerry—after scanning the book page quickly, to make sure that the advertisement of *Look Away, Stranger* had appeared on schedule—went back to the front page of the *Times*, and read of violent death.

Amanda Towne, whose picture did her credit, had been found dead, under circumstances the police characterized as suspicious, in a hotel suite occupied by Mr. and Mrs. Gerald North who, however, had an apartment of their own in Manhattan. (Why they were not in it remained unexplained in the *Herald Tribune*, although Inspector O'Malley was freely mentioned and his views, which were rather guarded, were fully quoted. If he had passed on the reason for the Norths' presence at the Breckenridge, that did not appear. Which, Pam thought, was needlessly mean of him.)

The exact cause of Amanda Towne's death had not been determined when the *Herald Tribune* went to press. But the *Times* had "apparently of asphyxiation." Miss Towne had a suite of her own on the same floor of the hotel—a corner suite, which the *Herald Tribune* considered "luxurious." The *Times* withheld comment. What she was doing in the wrong suite, and doing there dead, was the core of the matter. On this mystery, the Norths—it was reported—had been able to shed no light. The Norths, according to their account, did not know Miss Towne. The Norths, according to the police, said that they had gone out to dinner and the movies, leaving their suite empty—except for a Siamese cat—and had returned to find Miss Towne's body. They had reported this to the police.

"If I were somebody else," Pam said, when she had reached this point in the story, "I'd say those Norths are the ones who did it. A cooked-up story if I ever heard one."

"You," Jerry said, washing toast down with coffee, "you and Deputy Chief Inspector Artemus O'Malley, in command of detectives, Borough of Manhattan. All they need is a motive." He put his newspaper down briefly, so that he could look across the table at Pam. "You saw her show," Jerry said, thoughtfully. "Some of the shows you see make a person feel like—"

"It is not," Pam said, "anything to joke about. I don't see why we're not in jail."

"Give us time," Jerry told her, and went back to reading about Amanda Towne, of whom there was a good deal to write.

She had been in her middle forties, native of Arkansas, former newspaper woman in Chicago. She had been married, briefly, twenty years before, to Russell Barnes, then also a newspaper reporter—and now a copyreader (but copy editor in the *Times*) on an afternoon newspaper. According to Mr. Barnes, there had been no divorce; merely a friendly (and certainly protracted) separation. Mr. Barnes was shocked to hear of his wife's death. (And, therewith, more or less vanished from the picture.)

Amanda Towne had been living alone, and had resumed her maiden name, when she turned from newspapers to broadcasting. She had been first a newscaster on an afternoon radio program, her time period brief and her sphere news of interest to women. But she had not stayed there, or on the Chicago station which had given her a start. She went on to a half-hour period; to interviews as well as news—and to many glowing, dramatized, little reports on products of interest to women. She expanded further, became a network feature, and an institution and was an hour long and a nation wide. By this stage, her show had a name—"People Next Door"—originated in New York, where celebrities suitable to trial by interview are somewhat more easily come by.

"But what Amanda never did," her business manager, Mrs. Alice Fleming, assured the *Herald Tribune's* radio and TV authority (who had a separate story of her own, beginning on Page 1) "was to lose the common touch. She hated the word 'folksy,' of course, but I'm afraid it was often used of her. It was what made her appeal so universal. All over the country, women felt she was just—well, I guess, just the next door neighbor who had come in to call."

The transition from radio to television was somewhat difficult, and a good many—particularly among the women interviewers—fell between. Amanda did not; she kept a foot firmly on radio for longer than most, when radio dissolved under it, she was firmly on TV, from two to three, three afternoons a week, and was often asked, further, to give the woman's point of view on matters of world importance, Sunday afternoons being the most frequent times for this, since on Sundays television is most likely to think deeply.

"In recent years" (this was the *Times*' television commentator) "Amanda Towne became noted for the frequently penetrating quality of her questions, which sometimes drew forth revealing answers. In not a few cases, answers were somewhat more revealing than those interviewed realized. Her program was, through the years, often the source of news stories. The recent misadventure of Judge Roger Parkman is a minor example—although perhaps not particularly minor to Judge Parkman, whose political career, some think, has been jeopardized."

The *Times*' radio and TV man did not go further into that. The writer of the *Herald Tribune's* lead story did.

"Miss Towne," he wrote, "had a knack of making those she interviewed feel relaxed, as if they were talking with a sympathetic friend in privacy. It is said along Madison Avenue that some lived to regret what they had said in these relaxed moments, and to feel that Miss Towne had 'led them on.' An example cited is the very recent case of Judge Roger Parkman who, in the course of an interview with Miss Towne, made a casual remark which has been widely, if unfairly, interpreted as reflecting adversely on certain minority groups."

This, to the *Herald Tribune's* rewrite man, appeared to cover that, and he went to graze in other pastures. Pam read on, searching and not finding, and put her paper down on the table and said, "Jerry. This Judge Parkman?"

Jerry said, "U-mmm?"

"Parkman," Pam said. "Isn't it in the *Times?* What did he say that was so awful?"

"'—were varied,'" Jerry read. "'From the climbers of new mountains, to winners of cooking contests, from best-selling authors to—'"

"Parkman," Pam said. "Judge" (she checked) "Roger Parkman. Something he said has been widely interpreted."

Jerry marked his place with a finger. He said, "What did you say about Mr. Dulles?"

"Really," Pam said. "You never listen. Parkman. Judge Parkman. Something on Miss Towne's program. Isn't it in the *Times?*"

"Oh," Jerry said. "Yes. Something about—" He paused. He remembered. He said he remembered. He said it had been chiefly in the *Post*. Because Judge Parkman was a Republican. He'd been talked about for lieutenant governor or something. The rest of the papers had followed it with little enthusiasm.

"What?" Pam said.

"It wasn't anything much," Jerry said. "I do remember it was on Miss Towne's program. Perfectly innocent, anybody'd think. Only—" Pam waited while Jerry thought. "All he said," Jerry told her, "was something like 'people like you and me.' Or maybe, 'You and I and people like us.'"

Pam shook her head. She said it must have been the context.

It had been, Jerry said. He couldn't remember the context in any detail. But—relaxed, possibly led on—Judge Parkman had allowed himself to be netted in a context which made a probably innocent remark appear to reflect on all who were not, as he and Miss Towne triumphantly were, white and Protestant and, presumably, eligible for membership in the Daughters of the American Revolution. "On the distaff side," Jerry said, before Pam could say that a man couldn't very well be a daughter.

"Oh," Pam said. "In New York City. A politician. *And* a Republican. Ouch!"

In a word, it had been "Ouch!" Judge Parkman had been saying that, in statements of considerable length, since the previous

Friday, when he had spoken lightheartedly to the so sympathetic Amanda Towne—and to many thousands more, not all of them inclined to forbearance. There had been much pattering of little feet as Republicans from all around trotted forward to disavow Judge Parkman's implications; to say how deeply they, on the other hand, loved people of all races and all colors and all creeds. It had become entirely evident that Judge Parkman would not further be talked about for lieutenant governor. Or anything.

"The poor man," Pam said. "People should be very clear in what they say, shouldn't they?"

Jerry looked at her. He swallowed coffee. After consideration, he said, "Yes, Pamela."

"His career in shreds," Pam said. "And I suppose, nobody to sue? Since he said it himself. He must have been very annoyed at Miss Towne." She paused. "Very," she said. "Particularly if she led him on, as the papers say. Wove the context."

"Wove the—" Jerry said and paused to consider. Perhaps, on second thought, a context could be woven, and a career reduced to shreds thereby. It occurred to him, on third thought, that that, or part of it, might be precisely what Pam was doing.

"Listen," Jerry said. "He'd hardly be that annoyed, if that's what you mean." He lighted a cigarette and looked at it. "As," he said, "I suppose it is."

"Well," Pam said.

"What good would it do him?" Jerry asked. "The damage is done, presumably. Probably he can live it down. Anyway—"

Pam said she knew the one about frying pans and fires. To say nothing of least said soonest mended, and the rest. All the same—

"Suppose," she said, "he tried to get her to have him on the program again? So he could straighten things out? Say how much he loved minorities with votes? And she wouldn't do it? And he got mad and—"

"No," Jerry said.

"Somebody got mad," Pam pointed out. "Or frightened. Or stood to profit. I wonder if—"

"No," Jerry said. "This time, we won't try to help. All right? We sit this one out."

"If we're let," Pam said.

It was not precisely a promise. It would have, Jerry decided, to serve. He went to his office and Pam went back to the apartment, where the men of Prentori sized.

At a quarter of eleven, Jerry was talking, on the telephone, with an author about a bug, and being firm in his insistence that the bug would not go away no matter how little you looked at it. Miss Prentice, who received, came to the door of his office and her eyes were bright. "Try to think of something, Clem," Jerry said to the author. "Before we send it to the printer," and hung up and said, "Yes?" to Miss Prentice, who was clearly pleased and excited—as if the Book-of-the-Month had called in person, with entreaties.

"Mr. Kingsley would like to see you," Miss Prentice said, as one who imparts tidings almost too joyous for belief.

"Fine," Jerry said, and said thank you, and to ask Mr. Kingsley to come in and, to his secretary, "Better get the latest sales reports out, hadn't we, Jane?" Jane Whitsett thought they had indeed, and went for them.

They would, Jerry supposed, be what Byron Kingsley had come to see—to look at with that odd combination of pride and modesty and wonder which was so much part of him; to say, with that diffidence which, in spite of everything, was still so charming, that the figures were pretty good, weren't they, Mr. North? (Not quite saying, "Mr. North, sir," but somehow implying it.) He might also, of course, wonder whether it would be quite convenient to have a little further advance against royalties. Which would be all right. For the moment there was almost nothing Byron Kingsley could ask of North Books, Inc., which would not be all right. Mr. Kingsley was, to put it shortly, a publisher's dream. There had been no brighter dream since the man from Macmillan's took the manuscript of *Gone With the Wind* home in a trunk.

Byron Kingsley was, to put it even more shortly, the author of

Look Away, Stranger. Gerald North (president, editor-in-chief, of North Books, Inc.) still pinched himself awake when he looked at the sales figures of *Look Away, Stranger*. (Two other editors, who had turned it down, took Miltown tablets when they remembered.) It was that sort of thing, that sort of novel, and the whole business was still, Jerry admitted to himself at intervals, and to Pam now and then, entirely unaccountable. Lightning had struck. That was what it came to.

The manuscript of *Look Away, Stranger* had come, looking rather like a bale of cotton, out of Arkansas. It showed signs, already, of other journeys. Somebody had laid a cigarette, briefly, on page 6. Pages from 105 on were suspiciously fresh. No agent had intervened—there was the murky aura of amateurism plain around *Look Away, Stranger*, which was also something over six hundred pages in length.

Jerry had passed it down almost two years ago—passed it down as far as it would go, which was no great distance, since North Books, Inc., is not a Macmillan for size. "Have a look at this," Jerry had said, and the reader had sighed and said, absently, that he hoped it was typed on one side of the paper only.

"Deepest South I've ever dropped into," the reader had reported, orally. "Faulkner, Thomas Wolfe, touch of Williams. Old mansions falling into weed patches. And scions. Lots of scions."

"O.K.," Jerry had said, "put it over there somewhere," and it had been put over there somewhere, and stayed over there for a matter of weeks, looming large. Jerry forgot it; grew accustomed to its balelike bulk; saw it one day, for no reason in particular, and said, "Jane, have them bundle that up and—" He paused, for no reason in particular, and said, "No. Bring it—" and had looked at Jane Whitsett, a small, neat girl, and realized she would be no match for *Look Away, Stranger*, and got the manuscript himself. Got it and, to keep the franchise, to clear his conscience, read the first page. It was, at any rate, neatly typed. He read the second page, since conscience still pointed an accusing finger. And then he read the third.

It was all that the reader had said. It was Deep South. Moreover, it was a family chronicle, stretching from there to, it appeared at first glance, eternity. And yet—

Jerry took the first hundred pages home with him that evening, read late (having got around to it late) and was still on the far side of the Civil War. There had been a rape, of course—what Jerry presumed would be merely a preliminary rape. And a baby had fallen in a hogpen and, as was to be expected, been eaten. All of this was much as Jerry had foreseen, warned as he had been. And yet—

And yet, the next day, he found that, for reasons entirely obscure, he wanted to get on with it. He got on with it, as other things allowed. There were passages— There were scenes that—By page 300, Jerry found that, mentally, he was cutting; almost preparing for the printer. Although, of course, it would never come to that. It would—

"Read this damn thing," Jerry said, a week later, to Frank Barry, who was too good to stay much longer with North Books, Inc., unless it became Barry Books, Inc., or at the least North and Barry, Inc. Barry weighed it in his hands. He said it would have to be a five ninety-five book, at least. "Probably it won't come to that," Jerry told him. "But—"

There had been much editing, much cutting. This had been carried on by mail—carried on in long letters from Frank Barry, from Jerry himself, since they worked on it together; in short letters from Byron Kingsley, who was as brief in correspondence as he had been lengthy in art. Kingsley, from Arkansas—from, it appeared—a small town somewhere near Little Rock, had agreed at once that the book was too long; said he'd always known it was too long. He had been appreciative of acceptance, had signed a contract without demur, although Jerry (with conscience still pointing a finger) had suggested he might like to engage an agent; had said, to almost all suggestions, that they knew more about it than he did, and that he certainly was grateful for the help he was getting. He had behaved, indeed, gratifyingly unlike an author.

Jerry himself had worked on the book, with Barry, in a mood

recurrently one of misgiving. A good deal of the time, he was convinced that he was engaged in furthering the most colossal mistake of his life. Other and bigger firms (gossip gets around in the trade) had seen *Look Away, Stranger*, and shuddered, and looked away precipitately. "Warmed-over Faulkner" was the most common description gossiped; "Warmed-over Wolfe" was a close second. Probably older heads—and bigger pockets—had been right. And yet—

Look Away, Stranger was published in the early fall. It blew the top off. "I'm still damned if I know why," Jerry said, to Barry, and to Pamela North. "What's the thing got—?" He always ended that with a shrug. But it was nothing to be shrugged off.

Book-of-the-Month was part of it. A movie sale which, although his cut was small—conscience had shaken a finger angrily and been heeded—was something for Jerry to blink about, was a good deal of it. In addition to which, the trade sale (at $5.95) was a thing you had to look at to believe.

And there, finally—lured at last out of Arkansas—was Byron Kingsley himself and Kingsley was, in a fashion, as remarkable as the book.

Looking at him now, standing to greet him, Jerry North was once more startled by the magnitude of the phenomenon which was Byron Kingsley. There was, for one thing, the sheer size of the man. He was six feet four, a stature seldom attained by those who write for a living; he was solid from feet (in cordovan shoes, now) to thick and tawny hair. He had mild blue eyes in a wide and evenly tanned face; he was in all respects a singularly handsome man. But there was more to it than that—as there had been more to *Look Away, Stranger* than could be precisely evaluated. Like the novel, Byron Kingsley was, somehow, of more than life-size; handsomer than a man has any business being, yet inoffensively handsome. Perhaps because he gave no indication that he was in the least conscious of being handsome. Possibly that was the best thing about Byron Kingsley, at any rate from the view of people who wanted to make the best of him, and the best for him.

Now he stood, with just the faintest suggestion of a stoop (as a man who did not want the accidental advantage of greater height, and was embarrassed by it), and smiled (with just a touch of diffidence) and did not sit until Jerry had sat first. And then he said he hoped he wasn't butting in on anything, and that it was mighty good of Mr. North to let him barge in this way. He had a low, musical voice, and used it with charming diffidence.

Jerry, assuring him that he had butted in on nothing, could barge at will, remembered how, when Kingsley first came to the office—which was after Book-of-the-Month acceptance, when it became evident which way the wind blew—he had sat for almost half an hour in the reception room, in a corner out of Miss Prentice's view, and had merely waited patiently to be noticed. He might, Jerry thought, have sat there all afternoon, never thinking to rap on Miss Prentice's little window, call attention to himself, had not a stenographer, coming in from lunch, gone to Hilda Prentice with her eyes wide and her lips parted and enquired, "What is that wonderful thing out there?" Miss Prentice had looked, and taken steps to find out.

He sat now much as he had sat then, not putting himself forward. Two months of it had not changed him. His hair was better cut now; his clothes as urban as anyone's. But he was still as modest as he had been; as unhardened. For six weeks he had been interviewed, had been asked to speak—which he did diffidently, but surprisingly well—had been photographed. This had not changed him. He had had little (and somewhat obscure) anecdotes told of him in Leonard Lyon's column; had had parties given for him; had been able to read that no new writer of equal talent had appeared within memory. He still called all women "ma'am" and all men "sir." (It was not quite "suh.") Praised to his face, he tended to look uncomfortable and to say, "That's mighty nice of you, ma'am." (Or "suh.")

"Still snowballing," Jerry told him now. "See the ad in the *Times* this morning?"

Three columns, page depth, the advertisement had been. And

the book out almost two months. Jerry knew authors who would have embraced him.

"Mighty fine advertisement," Byron Kingsley said. "You're being pretty swell about the whole thing, sir. I hope it didn't cost too much, Mr. North."

Jerry North, who had thought Kingsley could no longer surprise him, steadied himself. He told Byron Kingsley not to worry about that. He said, "Look," and showed him the most recent figures. Byron Kingsley looked at them, and said he certainly owed Mr. North a lot. Mr. North, mentally, pinched himself. He was awake, all right, although it hardly seemed possible. Byron Kingsley leaned forward and carefully put the sales sheets back in front of Mr. North. He said he hated to take up so much time but—

"I'd sort of like to ask your advice, sir," Kingsley said. "Know I've been a lot of bother already to you and Mr. Barry. But—it's about this Miss Towne. The one who got—"

"Miss Towne?" Jerry said.

"I read about it in the papers," Kingsley said. "It's a pretty terrible thing."

"Yes," Jerry said. "I don't get—"

"They'd arranged I was going to be on her program," Kingsley said. "Miss Feldman made the arrangements."

"Oh," Jerry said. "Well, it's unfortunate. But they'll fix something else up. I'll ask Miss Feldman to come in and—"

"No," Kingsley said. "I mean, whatever you say, sir. But it wasn't so much about being on the program. You see, sir, I was there last night. Just before she got killed."

"You were—" Jerry said, and paused. "You mean, at the hotel?"

"In her room," Kingsley said. He looked at Jerry North, his expression compounded of anxiety and trust. "In her apartment, that is. She had what you call a suite. She—"

"You were there," Jerry said, accepting it. "Why?"

It was, explained, simple enough. Earlier in the week, after the date for Byron Kingsley's appearance on "People Next Door" had been set for Friday, Kingsley had been interviewed by a man from Miss Towne's staff—a man named Gray. Tony Gray, that was it. Gray had asked a lot of stuff—about his early life, and where he went to school and how he happened to write *Look Away, Stranger*, and what the title meant. "All that sort of stuff," Kingsley said. "Think he was going to write a book himself."

Kingsley had assumed that that finished it—that, with what Tony Gray had got, they would have more than enough background to provide questions, and answers, on the ten or fifteen minutes of conversation he would have with Amanda Towne. But Gray, leaving, had said that Miss Towne might think of some more things she'd want to know about. He had said that Miss Towne was thorough about things like that.

"They called me up yesterday morning," Kingsley told Jerry. "That is, Mr. Gray called me up and said, could I come around to Miss Towne's apartment that evening, about six-thirty, he said, because there were one or two things Miss Towne wanted to know more about. I said I would, of course. Though I sure thought by that time they knew about all there was to know. About me, anyway."

He had gone to Miss Towne's suite, getting there at six-thirty, punctually, and ringing the doorbell, and being let in by Miss Towne herself. "Thought there'd be somebody else there, it being her hotel room and all," Kingsley said. "But it was just Miss Towne. Mighty fine woman. Came from back home." He looked at Jerry North for response.

"Did she?" Jerry said.

"Talked like people back home," Byron Kingsley said. "Like I do, sir. Not so much, maybe, because she went away quite a bit ago. She was an older lady, of course. A little older. Mighty young looking, though."

They had talked, Kingsley said, for perhaps forty-five minutes. It had seemed to him that they went over the same things he had gone over with Gray, but if that was what she wanted he sure wanted to help out. Because he appreciated what Miss Towne, along with everybody else, was doing for him.

At about a quarter after seven, Kingsley said, the telephone had rung and she had talked to somebody, and had looked at her watch and said, "All right, if you like. In about ten minutes?"

He had said he'd taken a lot of her time, and maybe he'd better be going, if she had an engagement—and told her, again, that he sure appreciated the time she was taking.

"She said I was going to be fine," Kingsley said, "and to be at the studio early—one-thirty or about that, so they could see if I needed anything done to me. Makeup, I guess?"

"Probably," Jerry said. "Told you to wear a blue shirt, probably."

Kingsley looked at Jerry North with admiration, as one looks at the possessor of abstruse knowledge. That was just what Miss Towne had told him. And with that, he had left. At, he supposed, twenty minutes after seven, or thereabouts.

"And," Jerry said, "she was expecting somebody in five or ten minutes. There? Or was she going out to meet someone?"

"I don't know, Mr. North," Kingsley said. "Could have been either way, I guess. What I wanted to ask you—you think I ought to tell somebody about being there? If she was killed—" (It sounded a little, but only a little, like "kilt.") "I thought maybe I ought to, but then I thought, maybe it would be what they call bad publicity, and after all you and Mr. Barry have done . . . Anyway, I thought I better talk to you first."

He looked at Jerry, again with anxiety.

"She was all right when I left," he said. "You think they'd get the idea—?"

"No," Jerry said, and hoped they wouldn't, and wished, wholeheartedly, that "they" were anyone but Deputy Chief Inspector Artemus O'Malley. "That's absurd," Jerry said, firmly.

"You know who I ought to go to, sir?" Kingsley said. "In the papers it sounded as if you and Mrs. North had been—that is, as if you knew about things like this." He was circumspect.

Jerry looked at his big, gentle author, wondered momentarily where in him dwelt the knowledge, the sombre awareness of mankind's troubled life, which were reflected in *Look Away*,

Stranger. But he had wondered much the same about many authors, and found the speculation idle. They hid themselves, by intent or accident, behind many façades; they seldom looked, and often did not talk, like authors.

"Come on," Jerry said. "I'd better go along."

IV

PAINTERS ARE DEVASTATING; Pam North, huddled in the kitchen with Martini and Martha, was devastated. They had not yet reached the kitchen; it was a brief and precarious haven. It was also crowded, the kitchen being small and Martha large. The door to the rest of the apartment was closed, but the sounds of painters permeated everything, like the smell of paint. They conversed in hoarse shouts; they banged; it was clear that, for reasons of their own, they were tearing the apartment wall from wall. At intervals there were sounds of objects falling, and undoubtedly breaking into fragments.

Pam knew, kept telling herself she knew, that chaos did not really swirl beyond the closed kitchen door. She knew that, in some strange fashion, this noisy turbulence was only apparent; that, in reality, a kind of order prevails among painters. And that there were, after all, only three of them, plus Mr. Prentori, who stood in the center of things and, presumably, conducted. There were not twenty painters; there were not even a dozen painters. They were not, actually, armed with axes. They had lifted the mirror over the fireplace down in order that they might paint behind it. They had not chopped it down.

It is one thing to know; another to believe. Pam quivered inwardly.

"Now Mrs. North," Martha said, "you just quiet yourself. I'll make you a nice cup of tea."

"Laudanum," Pam said. "A nice cup of laudanum, well steeped."

"Just quiet yourself," Martha said.

"Ya—ow—*oo!*" Martini said, and threw up her breakfast.

A Miltown, Pam thought. That was the thing. A Miltown, which she would share with Martini. "It's all right, cat," Pam said. "It won't last forever."

"Yah-*ah!*" Martini said, wanting another breakfast.

"She'll just throw it up again," Pam said, when Martha, to whom Martini had spoken, asked a question with her eyebrows. "Her stomach is jumping up and down. The same way mine—"

The telephone rang. Far away, dimly, the telephone rang.

"Telephone's ringing, lady," Mr. Prentori shouted, apparently toward someone in Central Park.

Pam went. The living room was as she had imagined it. The mirror was gone. It did not seem to be anywhere. Presumably Mr. Prentori's men had thrown it out a window for safekeeping. The telephone rang again. Pam looked wildly around a room she had never seen before. In the center of the room there was a pile of something, with painty canvas over it. The telephone rang again, plaintively.

"Where is it?" Pam said, to Prentori. "*Where on earth is the damn*—the telephone?"

Prentori pointed. He pointed at the central mound, the painters' midden. The trapped telephone, rang plaintively—a telephone buried alive.

"Here," Prentori said, and pulled at the canvas. "Didn't want to get it all full of—"

There were chairs and small tables piled on a larger table. There was a vase on the top of the smallest table. It teetered and Prentori caught it. The mirror was on its face under the large table, cowering. The telephone was nowhere—yes, there the telephone was. At the far end of the pile, under the end of a sofa.

It rang again—it was exceptionally patient, for a telephone. Pam dropped to her knees; she wriggled in. "Watch the mirror," Prentori said, and she flattened herself and crept. Whoever it was would have—

She could just, by going half under the sofa, reach the telephone, get it out of its cradle. But she could not, for a moment, bring it to ear. From a distance, huskily, the telephone said, "Hello? *Hello?*"

Pam rolled over on her back, her head pillowed on the frame of the mirror. She got the telephone to her ear. She gasped into it.

"What?" a man's voice said. "Is this—?"

"The North apartment," Pam said. "This is—"

"Could I speak to Mr. North?" the man said. His voice remained husky; it sounded tired.

"Mister?" Pam said. "This is Missis. I'm afraid Mr. North—"

"—important I get in touch with him," the man said. "Very important. Is this Mrs. North?"

"Flat on her back under a sofa," Pam said.

"What?"

"Never mind. You wanted Mr. North? He's at his office, I'm afraid. Wait till I go around to the other side."

"I'm afraid—" the man said. "Is this the North apartment?"

"Wait!" Pam said, and wriggled out. Prentori looked down at her with pleased interest. "Oh," Pam said, and pulled her skirt down. She got up, and went around the midden, and pulled the telephone out on the other side. She could sit, now—sit on the floor, but sit.

"Let's start over," Pam said. "Who is this?"

"Don't know me," the man said. "Name's Barnes. It's important I get in touch with Mr. North. He's not at his office. They don't seem to know where I can reach him."

"Probably just gone to lunch," Pam said, and looked at her watch. It was a quarter of twelve, which made her suggestion seem unlikely.

"Or if they know they aren't saying," the man said. "Or when he'll be back. And I haven't got much time."

"Why?" Pam said. "What's it all—"

"Got to get back," the man said. "Can't tell through the switchboard. Tip the whole thing. See what I mean?"

"No. How could I?" She paused. "I'm Mrs. North," she said. "If there's a message?"

He appeared to consider this.

"Guess not," he said. "Pretty complicated. But—important. To him, as well. You've no idea?"

She had none.

"We've got painters," she said, feeling that something should be somehow explained.

"Tough," the man said. "Look—you're his wife—"

"Of course," Pam said.

"You can get in touch with him," the man said, in his husky voice. "I can't get away until about five. Come around there?"

"It's full of painters," Pam said. "Anyway—"

"All right," he said. "Meet him somewhere. Bleeck's? Bleeck's all right? It's damned important. If I'm right, it'll blow the roof off."

"The roof?" Pam said. It was the last thing she wanted. "You'll have to tell me more than—"

"Not now," he said. "Just tell him Barnes—Russ Barnes. And that it's as important to him as—"

"—for the next three minutes, please," the operator said.

"Barnes," the man said. "Bleeck's, around five. You'll tell him?"

"Well—"

And then the telephone clicked at her, and died in her hand.

"Well!" Pam said, to the dead telephone, and got up. Of all things. Whoever this Mr. Barnes was—

She stood up and looked at nothing. Barnes? Hadn't she heard, or read, something about a Barnes. In connection with—? Wasn't there a Barnes somehow mixed up—?

Barnes. Russell Barnes. The husband Amanda Towne had been separated from. Something important—too important for the telephone. Something that—what had he said?—would "tip the whole thing." (To say nothing of blowing the roof off.)

She retrieved the telephone. She dialed. She said, "Mr. North, please," and then, "All right, Miss Whitsett then. This is Mrs. North." Then she said, "Jane. I'm trying to get in touch with Mr. North. Is he out to lunch, do you think? Or—"

Jane Whitsett did not know. Mr. Kingsley had come in to see him, and Jane had gone off to her typewriter. Mr. North and Mr. Kingsley—even Jane Whitsett's voice vibrated slightly when it formed magic syllables—had gone out together; gone past her.

Jerry had said, "Back in an hour or so, Jane," but not where he was going.

"You've no idea?"

"No. Wait—just when they got to the door, Mr. North said something about West Twentieth Street. To Mr. Kingsley. About—wait—'have to go to West Twentieth.' I'm pretty sure that was it."

"Oh," Pam said. "Oh!" She pulled herself together. She thanked Jane Whitsett. She hung up.

"If it hadn't been for the painters," Pam explained afterward. "Or if I'd really taken Miltown or something, except that we haven't got any. Or if Teeney hadn't thrown up her breakfast, which always upsets me more than it does her. I was just—well, sort of frantic. Not myself, really."

"Of course not," Jerry said to that. Not that he was too sure. It was possible that, in reacting as she had, Pam had been very much herself. "I realize how you felt."

How, at that moment, she did feel was full of turmoil, of outrage. That Inspector O'Malley. That *impossible* man! To drag Jerry—Jerry the *lamb*—down there. As if he—he of *all* people—could have anything to do with— As if they hadn't already told everything they knew, as anybody with half a mind—a *quarter* of a mind—would have known just by—

"You'll have to do something else for a minute," Pam said to the painter in her bedroom. He was scraping plaster off the wall, onto the floor—onto everything—for reasons of his own. He was a small man on a ladder; he looked at her mildly. "While I get dressed," Pam said. He looked at her. Far as he could tell, she was dressed. Hard to tell what women meant by what they said. He came down the ladder and said, "All right, lady," mildly, and went out.

Pam changed quickly, in an atmosphere of plaster dust. In suit and stole—a pleasant by-product of death and decay in the Deep South—she went. "Two-thirty West Twentieth," she told a cab driver, that being the headquarters of the tenth precinct, and of the Homicide Squad, Manhattan West—that being, obviously, the place they had taken Jerry.

***

"—about twenty minutes before seven," Sergeant Stein said. "That's right, Mr. Kingsley?"

It was right.

"And she made an engagement, on the telephone, while you were there. For, say, about seven-thirty? Either there or somewhere else?"

That, too, was right.

"Probably there," Stein said. "Since she didn't allow herself time to go far. She didn't seem excited? Worried? Anything like that?"

"No sir," Byron Kingsley said. "I'm sure she didn't."

They, and Jerry North, were in a small and borrowed office, since in the squad room Sergeant Stein had only a desk among several desks.

Inspector O'Malley had not been at West Twentieth Street. He had gone downtown to Headquarters; he was expected to stop by Homicide West on his way to his office in the Fifties. This was all right with Jerry North; that was more than all right. Stein was a man one could talk to; a man who would listen.

"When she talked on the telephone," Stein said. "Did you get any impression, Mr. Kingsley? It's hard to be specific, of course, but—I mean did you feel she was talking to an old friend or, say, a business associate? To a man or to a woman?"

He smiled at Kingsley.

"Sort of thing a man like you might notice," he said. "At least, I'd think so. Part of your—" He paused and smiled again. "Trade, call it, to notice things like that."

"She was businesslike," Kingsley said. "So—not an old friend. I'm guessing. I—wait a minute. Let me think."

He put a fine, long-fingered hand to his jaw; rubbed his chin reflectively. (And looked, Jerry thought, rather like Rodin's "Thinker," if with more clothes on.) "Something seems just out of reach," Kingsley said. "Something I almost remember."

"Take your time," Stein said.

"'All right, if you like,'" Kingsley quoted. "'In about ten minutes'—and then, something else. "Like a name—I wasn't trying to listen. I was trying not to listen. You know? And she turned away, to put the telephone back." He shook his head slowly, his eyes a little narrowed. "Trying to remember," he said, and that seemed obvious to Jerry, to Sergeant Stein. "Wait," Kingsley said. "'Judd'? Could it have been 'Judd'?"

"Or," Stein said, as Kingsley looked at him, questioningly. "Or—judge?"

Then Kingsley nodded slowly.

"I can't swear to it," he said. "It could have been that."

"—instead of doing what you're paid to do." A clear voice, a high, excited voice, came from squad room, through door, into borrowed office. "Bullying people. Badgering people. Hauling people who've told you everything—and some things you didn't think to ask, too—down here at all hours of the day or night and—"

Stein looked at Jerry North. "Yes," Jerry said, "there's no doubt of it, sergeant. It's—"

"Wait a minute," a heavy voice, and a louder voice—and a voice full of excited rage—answered the other. With this voice, the door between seemed to tremble slightly. "Just wait a minute! What I do, young woman—"

"Don't call me that. As if I were—"

"Yes," Stein said. "Well—"

Deputy Chief Inspector Artemus O'Malley had come from a conference at Headquarters; a conference which had been unexpectedly agreeable. He had decided to stop by the squad headquarters to see how things went, in the matter of Amanda Towne and other matters. He had been, for a choleric man, in an unusually relaxed mood. He had encountered Mrs. North in the squad room. And Mrs. North was unrelaxed.

It had taken Inspector O'Malley several minutes to discover precisely what it was he had done which he was not supposed to do, and during those minutes his relaxation had ebbed. It had, indeed, not so much ebbed as rushed away, as if it had been held by a dam and the dam had collapsed.

He towered above Mrs. North; his rumbling voice dominated hers. (Which, after seconds, was one of the reasons he did not really understand what this was all about.) Another reason, of course, was that he had no idea whatever that Jerry North was in the office. He had told Mrs. North that.

"He's not here," he told her. "And if I do want him, I'll damn well send for him. You understand that?"

"Incommunicado," Pam North said. "You think I don't know? And if you're using lights, and rubber hoses, we'll make you—"

"Listen!" O'Malley yelled at that point. "If you think you and that husband of yours are immune to—"

"So you *are!*" Pam said. "Third degreeing. Because you don't know how to—"

Jerry took two quick strides to the door, and opened it, and said, "Wait a minute, Pam!"

"If you think for one minute—" Pam North said. "Jerry! What have they been doing to you? If this big Cossack has—"

"And what the hell," Inspector O'Malley said, "are you doing here anyway? Who sent for you?"

"Nobody," Jerry said. "And quit yelling at my wife, will you?"

"I'll yell at anybody I—" O'Malley said, and stopped, and took a deep breath. "Well, Mrs. North," he said, "see any bruises on him?"

"Having the nerve," Pam told him, "to deny he was here. When all the time—"

Stein appeared at the door.

"*Stein!*" O'Malley said, in a great voice, "did you bring these people here? *Did you?*" He paused momentarily. "I just want to know," he added, in a voice of jagged iron. "That's all I want to know."

"And," Pam said, "don't shout at Sergeant Stein, either."

O'Malley clutched his head.

"You two," he said, "get—*who might you be?*" This was to Byron Kingsley, who appeared behind Stein, who, on being spoken to said, "Well, sir, I—" in the mildest of voices.

Stein took his life—and he suspected his sergeancy—in his hand.

"This is Mr. Kingsley, inspector," he said. "An author who—"

"Author?" O'Malley said. "*Author?* You mean one of these guys who *writes?*"

"Yes," Stein said, quickly, to get that out of the way, to sweep it under a rug. "Mr. Kingsley had some information to give us. Very interesting information. Mr. North was kind enough to bring him along and—"

"Kind enough," O'Malley said. "*Kind* enough!"

"Well—"

"All right," O'Malley said. "You've got this—interesting information? Written down and signed?"

"Well," Stein said, "it's being typed."

"These—" O'Malley said, "these Norths? You need them any more?"

Stein shook his head.

"Then—" O'Malley said, and looked at Jerry North. He looked, also, more briefly, at Pamela North. He looked away.

"We were just going," Jerry said, and they went.

Fifteen minutes later, having duly signed—and thanked them all around, and hoped he had helped—Byron Kingsley went too. And then O'Malley came out of the office, which he had preempted, in which he had sought refuge, and said, "Come here, Stein."

Stein went there. O'Malley sat at the desk. He was eating a cigar.

"I'm sorry if—" Stein said.

"All right," O'Malley said. "O.K. Keep me filled in after this, but O.K. Weigand's in Washington?"

"With those fibers," Stein said. "Waiting for the FBI to run them through the—"

"I know," O'Malley said. "Sent him there, didn't I?"

It was a moot point. Stein did not raise it. He nodded.

"What I want," O'Malley said, "is you to go down there and do the waiting. Get it? And wire Weigand to get the hell back here. Tell him—" O'Malley paused. "Tell him his friends are lousing things up again. Tell him to get the lead out."

"Yes sir," Stein said.

"Tell him to fly," O'Malley said, and ate half an inch of cigar.

V

Both Norths reached Bleeck's, in West Fortieth Street, at a little before five. Pam went along because, as she pointed out, there was no place to sit down in the apartment, and because what Russell Barnes might have to say—if he was the husband of the late Amanda Towne; if what he had to say was connected with her death—concerned her as much as it did Jerry. "Suspects together," she explained. "Divided we fall. Also, I've no intention of letting you out of my sight, with that O'Malley around."

And this was quite unnecessary, since Jerry had all along assumed that she would go with him. They went past the bar, and Jerry nodded to an author of his who was clinging to it, and into the dark and pleasant, and then not heavily populated, inner room. They found a table and, since one does not sit empty-handed in a restaurant, drinks. They sipped, and watched the entrance to the inner room. There was, Jerry pointed out, only one trouble with it—they had no idea at all what Russell Barnes would look like, when he came.

"A newspaperman," Pam said. "A copyreader."

That was probable, Jerry agreed. If all newspapermen, subspecies copyreader, had a special way of looking, it could be assumed that Barnes would have it. But Jerry had no conviction that there were such special stigmata. And, in addition, a great many of the patrons of the Artists and Writers Restaurant, which is seldom called that, are workers on newspapers.

"He'll know us," Pam said. "Because our pictures were in the papers, except not very good ones, of course. But all we have to do is to look expectant. When the right kind comes in, by himself, we'll look expectant. That will do it."

The right kind began to come in, although most often not singly, at a little after five. The Norths sat and looked expectant, and sipped. When, at a quarter after five, they had sipped to bottoms of glasses, they ordered more. They continued to look expectant.

They turned expectancy on a heavy-set man in his middle years—Russell Barnes might be expected to be in them—who stopped in the passage between bar and inner room and looked around, in search of someone. He looked at them. Pam's expectancy brightened to a glow. He shook his head and turned and went back to the bar.

"It's possible," Jerry said, "that you're carrying it a bit too far. I'd rather not know what he thought."

"I've got to do it for both of us," Pam said. "You don't look expectant at all. Just sort of dazed. There's another. You do it, if you don't want me to."

Jerry looked, or hoped he looked as expectant as possible. The new one looked around the room, smiled and raised a hand and came toward them. Jerry moved forward in his chair, preparatory to getting up. The new one went past their table, his smile increasing, and joined the friends he had come to join.

"Ask somebody," Pam said, at five-thirty.

"Well," Jerry said, with doubt, but he went to the bar and asked the bartender. The bartender knew Russell Barnes. Barnes had not been in. Sure, when he came, he'd tell him where the Norths were.

"Hi, Jerry," the clinging author said. "What d'ja know?"

"Hi," Jerry said. "That your delivery date on the new one was two weeks ago yesterday."

"What you need," the author told him, "is a drink. That's what you need, boy. Give my friends here a—"

"No," Jerry said. "Thanks. Two weeks ago yesterday."

"What it is," the author said, "you think I'm just here pouring it down. And all the time, 'way down there, my subconscious is writing its head off."

"Fine," Jerry said. "Tell your subconscious what week it is, Charlie."

"You're a fine one," the author said, without animus, and

pushed his glass across the bar. Jerry went back to Pam. He shook his head. It was twenty of six.

"Newspapermen," Pam said, "have no sense of time. It's notorious."

They work to most exact times, Jerry pointed out. Their trade is one of timing.

"When they're not working, then," Pam said. "That must be him. Look expectant."

They looked expectant for a gray-haired man in his sixties. He looked at them thoughtfully; he came to their table. "Thought I knew you," he said. "Never forget a face. How've you been, Braithwaite?"

"Sorry," Jerry said. "Not Braithwaite. North."

"Sorry myself," the gray-haired man said. "Maybe it's names I never forget. Thought you were Braithwaite. Looked like you knew me, too."

"Sorry," Jerry said.

"Perfectly all right," the gray-haired man said. "Can't all be Braithwaites, can we?"

"It's nice to have that settled," Pam said, as the gray-haired man smiled cordially and left them. "Do you suppose he isn't coming?"

It had, now at almost six, begun to look as if Russell Barnes were not coming.

"But," Pam said, "he made it sound so urgent. Of course, my being under the sofa and everything—"

Jerry looked at her. He shook his head.

"Oh," Pam said, "when you think it's going to stop ringing before you get to it, you know it's urgent. Because afterward, if you don't, you'll be sure it was. So, if you do, you assume it *is* urgent. It's perfectly clear, really."

Jerry ran a hand through his hair. Their waiter, misinterpreting the gesture, said, "Yes *sir*," and went off to the service bar.

"Probably all it was," Pam said, "is that Mr. Barnes has a manuscript. *Jerry!*"

Jerry North jumped slightly.

"*There!*" Pam said, and pointed.

A lean man of medium height stood in the passageway between bar and room.

"*Bill!*" Pam said, and her voice carried. But he had seen them already, was smiling already and coming toward them.

He said, "Right, Pam," and sat down.

"You," Jerry told Captain William Weigand of Homicide, Manhattan West, "are supposed to be out of town. On another case."

"Right," Bill said. The waiter brought two martinis. "Thanks," Bill Weigand said, and took one of them. "What I call service." Jerry held up a finger to the waiter, who said, "*Yes sir,*" and went.

"Very good," Bill said, after sipping. "I was. I was called back. It seems the inspector—"

"He," Pam said, "has been very hard to get along with, Bill."

Bill Weigand grinned at her. He said he had gathered that—from Inspector O'Malley.

"We couldn't have been more co-operative," Pam told him, with a semblance of indignation.

"Your helpful selves," Bill said. "I know. The inspector found that he lacked time to give his full attention to the Towne case. Continue to supervise, of course."

"In other words," Jerry said, "he told you it was your baby. Did he say, 'It's a screwy one. Those Norths—'?"

"Right," Bill said. "In effect. You do seem to find rather more than your share of bodies, don't you?"

"It's not because we look," Pam said. "People just seem to—well, leave them around. Where we are—"

She stopped.

"I don't know," she said. "It's odd, a little. How did you know we were here? Waiting for a man who hasn't come?"

"I told Miss Whitsett," Jerry said. "In case something came up. Like O'Malley, for example."

"This man—" Bill began.

"Miss Towne's husband," Pam said. "He had something very

important to tell Jerry. Only—well, it's after six. And five was when he said, unless, because I was more or less under the sofa—"

"Wait, Pam," Bill said. "One thing at a time."

"Beginning with the sofa?"

"Any place," Bill said. "We'll put it in order later."

When she wishes, Pam can be as succinct as any, and clearer than most. Now she was both.

"You assumed," Bill said when she had finished, "that he wanted to get in touch with Jerry, as he put it, about Miss Towne's murder?"

"Wouldn't you? What else? I did think it might be only about a manuscript, but not really."

"Right," Bill said. "I would. But—why with Jerry? If he knows something, and wants to help, why not us? The police?"

Pam shook her head.

"He kept saying it was important to Jerry, too," she said. "As if—" She shook her head again.

It was conceivable, Bill thought, that Mr. Barnes might think he had something to sell the Norths. It was conceivable, but not likely. Unless—

"I suppose," he said gravely, "that Mr. Barnes didn't see you—er uh—smother Miss Towne? Want to be paid off."

"All right, inspector," Jerry said. "We'll go noisily."

Pam merely said that this was serious.

"Or," Bill said, "he might know something that would clear you. Might have seen you having dinner, sat behind you in this movie you say you went to."

"Went to," Pam said. "As you perfectly well know, if we say we did. Anyway, nobody really thinks we had anything to do with it. Not even O'Malley. You know that."

"Right," Bill said. "Not even the inspector. But all the same—important to Jerry. Something that would blow the roof off. As if—" He considered. "He thought finding out who killed Miss Towne would have some special interest for you two. Be of some special advantage to you. I suppose—"

He finished his drink. He said there was no sense sitting there supposing. He said he would be back, and went to a telephone. Pam spent the few minutes of his absence looking expectant, but nothing came of it, as she had not supposed anything would. Bill came back.

"Not at the paper," he said. "Nobody much is, now, since it's a p.m. Somebody's dropping around to his apartment."

"Mullins?"

"Mullins," Bill told her, "is familiarizing himself with the case. For both of us, as it happens."

"This judge," Jerry said. "The one she may have made the appointment with, if Kingsley heard her right. You know about that?"

Bill did. And former Judge Roger Parkman did, of course, leap to the mind. Former Judge Parkman would be given an opportunity to deny he had been talked to. Judge Parkman was already up to his lips in denials. One or two more would be child's play. All the same—

"It's pretty tenuous," Bill said. "Looks that way at the moment, anyhow. What damage there was was done. Killing wouldn't undo it. All he can do is to deny that what he said meant what it sounded like."

"Off the record," Jerry said, "did it? Mean what it sounded like meaning?"

"I don't know Judge Parkman," Bill said. "From what I hear—his subconscious probably sprang a leak."

"Or," Pam said, "was punctured." They looked at her. "By Miss Towne, of course," Pam said.

That was possible; almost anything was possible. What Bill wanted now was everything they could remember that might touch on Amanda Towne's murder, from the time they checked into the hotel until the police arrived. He knew they had been over it before.

"Over and over," Pam said. "The inspector doesn't absorb very well. However—"

They went over it together, pieced it together; again told everything, not forgetting Martini's pan of shredded newspapers, and her denial of access of it. They gave their theory as to how someone—Amanda Towne or her murderer—might have slipped into the suite while the maid was turning down beds in the other room, and hidden in the bathroom until the maid had gone out.

Bill Weigand said, "H-mm" to that, a little doubtfully. It would have been, he thought, taking a chance. Suppose the maid had returned to the bathroom.

"Well—" Pam said.

"Merely," Jerry said, "have pretended to be the one the suite belonged to. The maid wouldn't have known. He—or she—wouldn't even have had to use a name. In this case, our name."

Bill supposed so. It was unclear. Apparently, Amanda Towne had been killed in the North suite. Witness the lipstick smear on the pillow slip. It was, incidentally, definitely lipstick; it was of brand and color Amanda Towne had used.

"In her own apartment down the hall? It was down the hall?"

At the end of the hall; a corner suite. So far as Bill knew, nothing had been found there to indicate that Amanda Towne was killed there. That would be one of the things that Mullins, reading through reports, would catch them up on. "After all," Bill Weigand said, "I've only been on it a couple of hours."

"And," Pam said, "came right to us."

It had seemed the best place to come; the best starting place, since it had started with them. Bill finished his second drink. It was a little after seven, then.

"Eat with us?" Jerry said. "Here or anywhere?"

Bill thought not; he thought he would, if he could find him, pay a visit to former Judge Parkman, and listen to denials. That was a step, the next of many steps. He went; the Norths remained, ate substantially, debated whether to go home to paint or, again, to try a hotel.

"Home," Pam decided for them. "Paint or no paint. I've had enough of hotels, for the moment."

Bill drove his Buick, which had been parked somewhat illegally, through Fortieth toward Park—toward Park and the

Upper East Side and the house of former Judge Roger Parkman, who had become, within days, a former prospect for high office. Because, as Pam said, Amanda Towne had punctured his subconscious, occasioning a leak. Bill grinned to himself, and the radio spoke.

"Car X-one," the radio said. "Calling Car X-one. Come in please. Car X-one. Calling—"

"Car X-one," Bill said. "Weigand speaking."

The radio squawked. It squawked of death.

Bill turned down Park, instead of up. He used red headlights and, at Fourteenth Street, where traffic swirled sluggishly, he let the siren whine. Not that things wouldn't wait, not that there was any hurry, any more. But you got there as fast as you could, all the same.

"There" was Bank Street, well west; "there" was an area of elderly houses, converted to walkups; "there" was the third floor of one of the walkups—not much of an apartment, an apartment of worn furniture, and a good many books and magazines, and a typewriter on a bridge table.

A good many men were in the small apartment when Bill Weigand reached it. Murder draws a good many men.

Russell Barnes lay on the floor, near the small fireplace in the living room. His head had been beaten in. There was blood all over the poker with which—but not that day—he had stirred fires of cannel coal.

Mullins—Sergeant Aloysius Mullins—was one of the men in the little room. He stood and watched routine. He said, to Bill Weigand, that the inspector was sure going to love this. He said, "The Towne dame's husband, or ex," and pointed. He pointed to a framed photograph on a bookshelf. "The Towne dame," he said. "Ten-fifteen years ago, maybe."

Bill looked at the photograph—the photograph of a woman, and a pretty woman, with wide forehead and slightly pointed face, with lips parted in a smile and perfect teeth in evidence. So that was, had been, Amanda Towne. "She hadn't changed a lot," Mullins said. "Looks pretty much the same in the shots the boys took. Only dead, of course."

Bill Weigand nodded. He said, "O.K. now?" to a photographer, whose camera stared down at the dead man. "One more," the photographer said, and took one more, and said, "All right, captain." Bill crouched and looked at what had been Russell Barnes. He had been in his sixties, at a guess; his hair was gray and had needed cutting; his face was heavy and sagged somewhat, and he did not look as if he had been a particularly happy man. The face was untouched; he had been hit from behind, more than once. There was blood around the battered head.

He had not, Bill thought, been dead long—two hours, perhaps, or three. It was seven-thirty-five, then. "All right," a voice said. "Let's have a look at it."

Bill stood up and an assistant medical examiner crouched. His examination was brief; he looked up at Bill Weigand. "Two to four hours," he said. "Never knew what hit him."

"Right," Bill said, and watched the assistant medical examiner stand up, and rub his hands on a handkerchief. Bill stood, then, and watched—abstractedly—while prints were taken from dead fingers. He watched, but did not really see, the familiar routine. It was, he thought, rather lucky for Pam and Jerry North that Deputy Chief Inspector Artemus O'Malley was, for the moment, merely supervising. O'Malley was a man to put two and two together, and frequently come up with a lot.

Not Judge Parkman now. Judge Parkman could wait. The machine was working—a man sketched the room quickly, with chairs and worn sofa and body noted; the print men dusted; a lab man waited with a vacuum. The machine would carry the body off to the mortuary at Bellevue and all it wore and carried would be scrutinized, as the body itself would be scrutinized. The machine did not need Bill's help, or anyone's guidance. It would, in time—and not much time—produce reports.

"Come on," Bill said to Mullins, and they went on. They sat for a moment in Bill's car.

"It's going to be a screwy one," Mullins said.

"I know," Bill said. "The Norths are in it. You want to go talk to Judge Parkman? Let him say he didn't do it?"

"O.K., loot," Mullins said. The habit of years stuck; with others absent, Weigand would always be "loot," promotion notwithstanding.

Bill dropped Mullins at the Fourteenth Street station of the West Side IRT. Bill found a telephone. He found the number of the *Globe-Dispatch* and dialed and waited until a male voice —a young male voice, but weary for all that—said, "Globe-Dispatch."

"I'd like to talk to somebody in the city room," Bill said. "The city editor?"

"Nobody there," the young voice said, with greater weariness. "This is an afternoon paper, mister. Mr. Perkins goes off around five. Around six, everybody goes off."

"Perkins," Bill said. "He's the city editor? He'd be the one to talk to about a copyreader?"

"Depends on what—who is this, anyway?"

Bill told him.

"Gee." The young voice was no longer weary. "Something we ought to—"

"You will," Bill told him. "Where can I find Mr. Perkins?"

"We're not supposed—" the boy said, and hesitated. "You're sure you're the police?"

Bill was.

Paul Perkins, city editor of the *Globe-Dispatch*, lived in the Murray Hill district. He had a telephone, number not listed but provided. His answering voice was clipped, precise. Bill told him, briefly, what there was to tell. Paul Perkins would be damned. He would certainly talk to Captain Weigand.

He opened the apartment door to Captain Weigand ten minutes later. He was in his early forties; he was a neat, quick man with a crew cut. He took Bill Weigand into a large, comfortably furnished, living room. A dark-haired woman stood by a sofa. "Police captain, Myra," Perkins said. "My wife, captain."

"Weigand," Bill said, and, from somewhere else, a child said,

"*Mama!*" Myra Perkins shrugged, with a kind of gentleness, and smiled, and went.

"Drink?" Perkins said, and Bill shook his head.

"It's a hell of a note," Perkins said. "Poor old guy. Why?"

They didn't know; they would find out. Did Perkins know any reason why Russell Barnes, former husband of Amanda Towne, should, within hours after his wife's death, find it important to see Gerald North, of North Books, Inc.?

"No," Perkins said, crisp and precise.

"Nothing concerned with the paper?"

"No. Barnes is—was—a copyreader. On the rim. Good reliable man. Needed a day off now and then to sober up. Not a fast man—and didn't railroad copy, as some of them do."

"I take it," Bill said, "that he wouldn't be working on a story?"

"No," Perkins said, and qualified. "Not that I know about. Not assigned to anything—wouldn't be, of course. Reads what comes across the desk. Spells for those who can't. Puts in punctuation. Sees that things make sense. Writes headlines."

"I know," Bill said.

"Used to be a reporter," Perkins said. "Most of them used to be, you know. Been around a long time, Russ had. Chicago. St. Louis. Kansas City. All over the lot." Perkins considered. "The old-timers got around, generally," he said.

"Mine, mama," a child's voice said, from somewhere. It was not the same child's voice, Bill thought.

"Two of them," Perkins said. "Six and eight. We don't get around so much nowadays. Generally. You think Russ's death ties in with his wife's?"

"Right," Bill said. "Wouldn't you?"

Perkins would.

"You're sitting on it?" he asked.

"No."

"On the a.m.'s time," Perkins said. "Our man, their story." He shrugged. "You want to know what I know about him, I suppose? I don't know what he was up to. Why he wanted to get in touch with a publisher. Shouldn't think he'd have a book up his sleeve." He considered. "Of course," he said. "You can't always tell. Sure you won't have a drink?"

Bill shook his head. He listened to clipped words, to facts precisely ordered.

Barnes had been about sixty-four or sixty-five. The office records would fix it. He had worked for the *Globe-Dispatch* for about four years, always on the rim of the copy desk. He worked from eight to four-thirty five days a week. He got a little better than the Guild minimum. He was steady—except for his infrequent hangovers—not outstanding. Now and then, when he got a story he liked, particularly one that had the "light touch," he wrote a headline which was out of the ordinary. He was friendly enough with the rest of the staff—even with the rewrite men—but not especially friendly, so far as Paul Perkins knew, with any.

"He called Mrs. North about a quarter of twelve," Bill said. "He'd have been on his lunch hour?"

"Probably," Perkins said. "You'd have to ask Cliff. He's the slot man." He looked at Bill. "Runs the copy desk," he amplified. "Probably Barnes goes—went—off about eleven-thirty, after the makeover goes in. Supposed to take half an hour."

"He said he didn't want to call through the switchboard," Bill said. "I suppose he meant the office switchboard. 'Tip the whole thing off,' he told Mrs. North. Does that suggest anything?"

It did not. The girls might listen in. They seldom had time enough. He could think of no reason they should listen in. Still—one never knew.

"What would he tip?" Perkins asked.

Bill didn't know. Perkins had mentioned Chicago as a place Russell Barnes had worked. What did Perkins know of those days?

"Hearsay," Perkins said, and amplified. There were—had been more often in the old days—certain newspapermen of whom most other newspapermen had heard. The old-timers. Often, Perkins thought, remembered as more than life-sized—the Paul Bunyans of the trade. Barnes had been one of those, twenty years before, twenty-five years before. Chiefly in Chicago. A top man, getting top stories. Briefly, Perkins thought, a correspondent during the first World War. One of the "old Chicago crowd." Perkins did not know how deeply one. A reputation for brilliance. Perkins did not know how justified.

It was in those days, apparently, that he had married Amanda Towne, who must have been a girl just starting in.

"At a guess," Perkins said, "she must have been twenty years younger. You'd think so?"

"About that," Bill said.

"He never talked much about her," Perkins said. "Not to me, anyway. He never talked much to me about anything, as a matter of fact. I gather they were separated, not divorced?"

"Apparently," Bill said. "What happened to Barnes? To—rub off the luster?"

"I suppose," Perkins said, "he just got older, don't you? They used to talk about newspaper work being 'a young man's game.' But then, what isn't, come down to it? I wish I knew, don't you? Of course, he may have drunk too much. He didn't with us. Just—slowed down, I guess."

"After he and Miss Towne separated?"

"I don't know. It could be. Or maybe she, being a lot younger, slowed him down. Hard to keep up with people twenty years younger sometimes, especially when you're married to them. At least, I suppose it is. Not a thing I've ever tried. Get tired running to keep up, wouldn't you think?"

"Right," Bill said. "You don't know whether he and Miss Towne saw much of each other? Recently, I mean?"

Perkins shook his head.

"She could have called him at the office? Or he her, of course?"

"Sure. Why not? You think she could have told him something—who was going to kill her, say?"

Bill grinned at that, briefly. He said he didn't know what to think, at the moment. He said, at the moment, he was just poking around. If Mrs. Barnes had called her husband, at the office, would anybody be likely to know about it? Remember it? If, say, she got the switchboard and said, "I'd like to speak to Mr. Barnes, please. This is Amanda Towne calling."

Perkins considered. He supposed, if it had been like that, one of the girls on the board might remember. Since almost everybody had heard, if only vaguely, of Amanda Towne.

"To get him," Bill said, "she would—do what? The switchboard girl, I mean. He wouldn't have a special extension?"

"Call the copy desk," Perkins said. "Probably Cliff would answer. Say, 'Call for you, Russ.' "

"Cliff—what's the rest of his name, by the way?"

"Clifford Cohen," Perkins said.

"Would Mr. Cohen remember?"

Perkins doubted it. He might. But, if she had called—he supposed Weigand meant recently—what?

"I haven't the least idea," Bill said.

"And," Perkins pointed out, "they're both dead."

There was no doubt of that.

"Look," Perkins said. "This is going to be quite a story. He was our man. Do we get a break of any kind? A—slight leak here and there?"

"Officially—" Bill said, and let it hang.

"Of course," Perkins said. "I realize that. However?"

"It is hard," Bill said, carefully, "to say what might come up, Mr. Perkins."

Perkins said he would settle for that. He said Cliff Cohen lived up in Riverhead, if Captain Weigand wanted to talk to him. He said he could easily have one of the boys talk to the telephone operators. "No," Bill said, "we'll do it. You've got Mr. Cohen's number?"

Perkins had. He would do more; he would try to get Cliff on the telephone, pave the way. He did. He said, "Cliff there? Paul Perkins," and waited and said, aside, "Kid always answers the telephone at Cliff's place." He said, "Cliff? Russ Barnes was killed tonight. Chap here from the police—Captain Weigand—'d like to ask you a question."

He held the telephone out. Bill asked the question. "When?"

Clifford Cohen asked, and spoke like Princeton. Bill did not know. The day before; any time in the last few days.

It seemed to Clifford Cohen that he did remember, vaguely. Yesterday? He thought, probably, Tuesday. A woman had called, he did remember that, now. He had handed the telephone to Barnes, who had stood up and turned away from the desk, for privacy. It was Cohen's impression that the call had been short; his even vaguer impression that it had ended with Barnes saying something like, "I'll call you back." He had no idea whatever whether the caller had been Amanda Towne. He was sorry he couldn't help more.

"It doesn't get you much of anywhere, does it?" Perkins said, and Bill admitted it didn't get him much of anywhere. But—

He thanked Paul Perkins. After a moment's consideration, and in answer to a question, he said it was perfectly all right if the *Globe-Dispatch* mentioned the telephone call, speculated on its source.

Bill drove back to West Twentieth Street. Inspector O'Malley wanted him, on the double. He had been a little afraid of that. He drove uptown to borough command headquarters.

VI

Behind his desk, Deputy Chief Inspector O'Malley looked choleric. When he spoke, he proved choleric. Bill had expected this, if not looked forward to it. Inspector O'Malley is not, at best, a man of even temper. Association with Mr. and Mrs. North, even, as now, at one remove, does not put him at his best. And there was, Bill gloomily thought, more to come.

"All right," O'Malley said, "what've you got?"

Bill had two dead people; had husband and wife dead. O'Malley knew that.

"Nothing conclusive," Bill told him. "Miss Towne—or Mrs. Barnes—was definitely smothered. Barnes was beaten to death. With a poker."

"I can read," O'Malley said, and gestured toward reports on his desk. "What've you got, man?"

Reporters had been after O'Malley. That was clear. His allergy to reporters is second only to his allergy to Norths. What Bill had, and had now to tell, was not calculated to mollify.

"Barnes was trying to get in touch with Mr. North today," Bill said. "Around noon. Was to have met him at—"

He stopped. O'Malley had half risen from his chair. His red face seemed to expand.

"*North!*" he said, profanely. "Every time anybody turns around—" He subsided into his office chair. It was painful to see his effort at control. Probably, Bill thought, his doctor had advised. "Remember your pressure," his doctor probably had said. "Don't let things get you."

"Why?" O'Malley said, his voice leaden with calm. "Just tell me why!" But he shouted the last.

"North doesn't know," Bill told him. "It seems Barnes talked to Mrs. North first and—"

O'Malley gripped the edge of his desk. Bill waited for the paroxysm to pass.

"Don't," O'Malley said, "tell me what she said he said. Just don't, Bill."

It was entreaty, reinforced by the familiarity of Christian name. It was man to man.

Bill did not. He summarized. He told of the wait of the Norths at Bleeck's, of Barnes's failure to appear—nothing of Pam's having been under, or partly under, a sofa. He spared O'Malley as he could.

O'Malley's face did not lighten, but he began to nod his head; Bill had expected that; been afraid of that. O'Malley was, for some seconds, silent when Bill had finished.

"All right," he said, then, and kept reason in his tone. "You see it. Friends of yours or not, you see it. What have you done about them?"

"Left them ordering dinner," Bill might have said. "Nothing," he did say.

"Nothing," O'Malley said. "*Nothing!*"

Bill waited.

"Listen," O'Malley said. "A woman gets killed. Right?"

"Right."

"Shut up a minute. *Listen!* Her husband gets killed. Only, before he gets killed, he calls up a man—call the man Jones if you want to. Say he isn't—" O'Malley paused. "Say he's just anybody. Tells this man—call him Jones, like I say—he's got something important to see him about. Important to this man Jones. Call him Jones. You with me?"

"Right," Bill said.

"And," O'Malley said, and leaned forward over his desk. "*And*—it's in this man's room—this Jones man's—the other man's wife gets killed. You with me?"

Bill was.

"So what," O'Malley said, "does this man Barnes want? What's he know that's so important to Mr. North? You're a cop

—supposed to be a cop. Say it's just a man named Jones." He considered that for an instant. "North is, I mean," he said.

"I know what you mean," Bill told him.

"Barnes was to meet North at five. That's what North says. North and—and Mrs. North—go to Bleeck's to wait. Barnes doesn't show. You think they were surprised?"

"Yes," Bill said. "I do, inspector."

O'Malley clutched his head in his hands, to hold it in place. "You're not dumb, captain," he said. "Anyway, I hope you're not dumb. A shakedown. Want me to spell it?"

He would, anyway. Bill nodded.

"Barnes knows something about his wife's getting killed," O'Malley said, patiently. "Knows North killed her. Probably knows why. All this malarky about not knowing what he wanted. That's—malarky. North knew, well enough. Knew where he lived, too. Went down there—this Bleeck's business is eyewash. Decided it was a better idea to bash his head in than to pay what Barnes wanted. *Bashed* his head in. Went up to Bleeck's and put on this waiting act. With his wife. Well?"

"You think Mrs. North went along?" Bill asked. "To help kill Barnes?"

"How the hell," O'Malley enquired, "would I know, Weigand? Do I have to do everything? Wait a minute." He shuffled through the papers on his desk; found the one he wanted. "Two to four hours, the M.E. says. Says that at about seven-thirty. So Barnes could have been killed at three-thirty. Plenty of time for North to get to Bleeck's."

"Plenty," Bill said.

"They got there at five," O'Malley said. "Who says that?"

"They do."

"Who else?"

"I didn't ask anybody else. Right. I got there at six or thereabouts. They could have got there only fifteen minutes earlier, instead of an hour earlier, as they said. The round of drinks they were getting could have been their first, not their second, as I assumed. So they could have killed Barnes as late as five, or five-fifteen, and been at the restaurant when I got there."

"Now," O'Malley said, "you make sense, Bill. Now you do."

"And," Bill said, "if North killed Barnes at five, say, or a little before, and got blood on his clothes, as he might have, he'd have had time to go home and change before he went to Bleeck's."

"*Now* you're making sense," O'Malley told him. "Like a cop should. So now—what?"

Bill took a deep breath.

"Now," Bill said, "nothing, inspector. Nothing about the Norths."

O'Malley merely glared. He was beyond words.

"They had nothing to do with either murder," Bill told him, and watched the red face redden.

"Says who?" O'Malley asked. "Says you."

"Yes," Bill said. "Oh—I'll have the restaurant checked out, if you say so. Find out they got there at five, as they said. I'll ask Jer-Mr. North if he happened to kill Barnes and not mention it."

"You," O'Malley said, "will bring them in."

It had come to that. There had always, Bill thought, been a time it would come to that.

"No," he said. "I won't, inspector. You can take me off the case. Sure. You can get somebody to bring them in. Sure. You can put me back in uniform, and bring departmental charges and a lot of things. But—the Norths never killed anybody and never will."

"And," O'Malley said, "they're friends of yours. Why don't you say that, Weigand?"

"Right," Bill said. "And they're friends of mine."

"They're screwy," O'Malley said. "They keep cats. They're in the middle of this thing. A woman goes in the Norths' room and gets killed. A man's got something important to tell them and gets killed. And—they're friends of yours! Well?"

"Right," Bill said, and waited.

"You," O'Malley said, "are a damn fool."

"Possibly."

"And you sit there—" He looked at Bill Weigand, who had stood up, now it had come to this. "You stand there and I order you to bring them in for questioning, or suspicion of homicide or—hell—material witnesses. And what do you say, captain? You say no."

"I," Bill Weigand said, very quietly, "say 'no,' inspector."

"I bring charges. I put you in uniform. Hell—I get you thrown off the force. Where you've been a hell of a long time. You don't want to be a cop, Weigand?"

"I want to be a cop. You can do all those things. The Norths don't kill."

And then O'Malley leaned back—leaned far back—in his office chair and looked at Weigand; looked at him with sharp blue eyes half shut in the red face.

"You stake a lot," he said, and his voice—for O'Malley's voice—was low, "on these screwy friends of yours."

"Right."

"You're a damn fool."

They went in circles. "Possibly," Bill said.

O'Malley closed his eyes entirely. He took a deep breath into his massive chest. And then, as if from a great way off, but quietly—for O'Malley very quietly indeed—he said, "What do you plan to do next, captain?"

"Find out what Mullins got from Judge Parkman," Bill said, as quietly. "Talk to people at the broadcasting company. Get what I can out of Chicago. I'm still on it, then?"

O'Malley opened his eyes.

"Don't," he said, "be a damn fool, Bill. You think I'd expose anybody else to these—these friends of yours? With the whole department understaffed already?"

He leaned forward over his desk.

"Only," he said, "you'd better be right. It'd be tough all around if you turned out wrong. Why Chicago?"

"Barnes came from there. At least, worked there for some time. Probably married Miss Towne there. I talked to the city editor of the *Globe-Dispatch*. Man named Perkins. What I got was—"

Bill sat down again. O'Malley listened.

***

Pam North wriggled across the seat and wriggled out. Jerry closed the cab door and the cab flicked off, and Pam looked after it resentfully. "The small economy size," she said. "How I hate them. Remember when they were big enough to get into? And, out of?"

Jerry did.

"More runs," Pam said. "Every time I get in one I get runs. Unless, of course, I get them when I get out. In stockings."

Jerry had supposed in stockings. He said so. It was a pleasant evening, as November evenings go in New York—it was not actually raining, and there was only a moderate fog; the air, a stimulating mixture of gasoline fumes and coal smoke, barely stirred. There was hardly enough wind, indeed, to blow discarded newspapers along the gutters. "New York in the fall," Pam said. "And small economy-size cabs. And—"

A man loomed—a big man, wearing a camel's-hair coat; his tawny head bare. He said, "Hi, folks," in a low and musical voice—a voice which had in it, at the moment, a note of mingled pleasure and what Pam took to be embarrassment. He smiled down at them—he smiled down at almost everyone—with diffidence, as if he might have intruded; as if, indeed, they might well tell him to go away.

"Why," Pam said, "Mr. Kingsley."

"Just taking a walk," Byron Kingsley said, in the tone of one who hopes it will be all right with everybody. "Not been down in this part of town yet and heard a lot about it, ma'am. Evening, sir."

"It isn't what it used to be," Pam told him, as people have for years been telling other people about the area of Manhattan still known as the Village. "All built up, now. See?"

She indicated the apartment house in front of which they stood; the apartment house the Norths lived in. "When we were first here," Pam said, "it was only four stories and on top there was a studio. With a painter, sometimes."

"It's sure grown, ma'am," Kingsley said, looking up at it. It went up many stories now; it had setbacks and balconies.

"It sure has," Pam agreed and then, because it occurred to her that Byron Kingsley might feel that he was being—how would he put it himself? Teased? Even condescended to?—said, quickly, "They tore the other one down, of course. First."

"Yes, ma'am," Kingsley said. "Still mighty interesting down here. Different, sort of. Well, you all don't want to stand here. It's right cold."

"Why," Pam heard herself saying, "don't you come up and have a drink, Mr. Kingsley?"

Kingsley said, "Well—" and looked at Jerry North who said, with what conviction he could manage—more, at that, than Pam had expected—"Sure. Good idea."

Kingsley said, "Well—" again, in the tone of one who now, surely, intrudes. Then he said it was mighty nice of them.

"Of course," Pam said in the elevator, "the apartment's an awful mess. Painters. But anyway—"

The elevator stopped; Pam led the way down the corridor. Jerry opened the door and the odor of paint rushed out to meet them. Martini attempted to rush out also and was blocked by a foot. She spoke of this, bitterly, but then retreated into the living room and rolled to her back, legs softly crooked in a pleading position. Pam crouched and rubbed her belly. She told her she was a nice cat, a beautiful cat. She lifted her into arms and said, "And you smell of paint like everything." At which, Martini purred for a moment, and then wriggled. Pam put her down.

"Mighty pretty cat," Kingsley said, obligingly, in his soft voice. And then Martini crouched and laid her ears back. He reached down to touch her and she backed away and hissed. And then she ran.

"Gee," Kingsley said, "I'm sorry. I do something wrong?"

"Strangers," Pam said. "I thought she'd outgrown that. It's probably—I don't know. She hates things to be upset and there've been painters. It's—" She looked around the room. Most of the furniture was still in the painters' midden, with canvas over it. "Perhaps Jerry's room," Pam said. "Or the bedroom."

Jerry's room was occupied by that part of the living room furniture which was not in the midden. The bedroom contained beds and an accessible chair or two. Jerry threaded his way to the liquor cabinet, excavated it; made drinks. "Mighty good bourbon," Kingsley said. "Looking at you, folks."

They looked. They sipped. Silence intervened. Pam was tempted to ask Kingsley if he had written any good books recently, and resisted. Jerry was tempted to look at his watch, and resisted. Kingsley was not, apparently, tempted by anything at all, except possibly by bourbon. After a time, he repeated that it was mighty good bourbon.

"Except," Pam said, "that everything tastes of paint."

"Don't mind it," Kingsley said. "Mr. North—I do all right?"

"Do all right?"

"With the police," Kingsley said. "You know what I mean?"

"Oh," Jerry said. "Fine." And wondered what on earth his author did mean, and reminded himself that North Books, Inc., had never had another such author and—

"—in the papers," Kingsley was saying.

"It's likely to be," Pam said, proving that she, at any rate, had been listening. "If the police tell them, of course. But don't worry about it, Mr. Kingsley."

"Back home," Kingsley said, "people would think it was sort of funny. My being in her room and everything. And then her being killed."

He shook his head at his glass, which was still largely full.

"Everybody's been so swell," he said. "I'd hate to throw a monkey wrench into the machinery. I'd sure hate to do that, sir."

"Forget it," Jerry said. "Nobody'll think anything about it."

"Bad publicity," Kingsley said. "I'd hate that to happen. But I had to tell them. I don't suppose it did any good but—you say I did all right? Didn't give them any—wrong ideas?"

"You did fine," Jerry said. "Nothing else you could have done. Don't worry."

That was it, Kingsley told them. He had been worrying. He couldn't help worrying. He spoke slowly, still diffidently. He said that it was probably hard for them to realize how—how prodigious all this had been for him.

"You come out of a small town," he said. "Nobody—thinks much of you. Except, maybe, that there's something queer about you because—well, because you write, instead of farm, or work in a store. And then—all this. You see what I mean? People writing about you, wanting to interview you on TV. Inviting you to things." He looked up at them and smiled and Pam thought, He's sweet, really. And, under it—how much more he must be, to write as he does. You wouldn't think it, Pam thought.

"What it comes to," Byron Kingsley said, "I'm just a country boy, I guess. I've come what they call a far piece. I'd—well, I'd sure hate to have anything spoil it. You think this won't, Mr. North?"

"Of course not," Jerry said. "Just interest people more, if anything." He thought of trying to explain to this man from the country—this greatly talented, oddly simple and immensely valuable author of his—that, for people of a certain sort, in a certain category, almost no publicity is really bad. (Unless, of course, it can be publicly alleged that they read *Das Kapital* in youth. It seemed somehow unlikely that Byron Kingsley had.) "Don't worry about it," Jerry said again and this time he did, in spite of himself, glance at his watch. Jerry likes his sleep; the previous night had given him little. It was, to be sure, only a few minutes short of ten o'clock.

If Kingsley observed Jerry's surreptitious glance, he did not reveal it. He nodded at his drink again and sipped from it—a big, gentle man, reassured in a strange world. He said he'd try not to; that he was glad he had bumped into the Norths, because he had been worrying. He looked up. He said, "It's a strange thing. Why would anybody want to kill a fine woman like that?"

The Norths did not know.

"I wonder," Kingsley said, "whether they—the police, I mean—are getting anywhere?"

"They're very good," Jerry said, a little vaguely. "I—"

"Why don't we listen?" Pam said. "We can't look, because the TV is under things. But—" She leaned down to turn on the bedroom radio, on a shelf under the night table. The radio said nothing for a few seconds. Then it made preliminary scratching sounds. Pam, who had been lying on the bed, leaned from it—at some risk of falling under it—and twisted knobs.

"—o'clock news," the radio said, in an authoritative, deep voice, "James Fergus reporting. First, a quick look at the weather. Rain is expected beginning late tonight and continuing tomorrow, probably becoming mixed with snow in the northern suburbs. We will have the complete weather report at the end of the broadcast. In a moment, a spectacular development in the continuing investigation of the murder of Amanda Towne, famed star of the Continental Corporation's network. But first, a word about Supercal. Have you—"

"Fergus," Pam said. "Fergus. Oh—he was the announcer on her show. It must be difficult for him to—"

"Shhh," Jerry said.

"It's just about Supercal, whatever that is," Pam said. "It's bad enough to have commercials without listening to—"

"Pam!" Jerry said. "Shush!"

"—I'll spell it for you," the radio said. "S-u-p-e-r-c-a-l. The combination of ingredients recommended by four out of five doctors for—"

"I have always," Pam said, "wondered about the fifth one. Shot him, prob—"

"Pam!"

"And now the news. Less than twenty-four hours after the discovery of the body of Amanda Towne, famed TV personality and valued colleague of all of us here at the Continental Broadcasting Corporation, her estranged husband was found murdered this evening in his Greenwich Village apartment. According to police, Russell Barnes, Miss Towne's husband and an employee of a New York newspaper, was beaten to death, apparently with a poker. Police believe the two deaths are connected."

Nobody—not even Pamela North—interrupted James Fergus now. Byron Kingsley leaned toward the radio; Jerry North was, now, far from sleep.

"As most of you will recall," the radio said, in the deep, steady voice, "Miss Towne's body was found last night in a suite of a midtown hotel occupied by Mr. and Mrs. Gerald North. Mr. North, a New York publisher, and his wife, have denied any knowledge of her death and this has, apparently, been accepted by the police. The police have now established definitely that Miss Towne was smothered, apparently by a pillow pressed down on her face.

"However, Deputy Chief Inspector Artemus O'Malley, in charge of the investigation of both deaths, says that Barnes appears to have had an appointment with Mr. North for late yesterday afternoon—an appointment he failed to keep. Mr. North, according to Chief O'Malley, asserts that Barnes had arranged the appointment in a telephone call, saying it was important. But Mr. North denies having known Barnes or any knowledge of why Barnes wanted to see him. Stay tuned to this station for further reports on this rapidly developing case.

"Now, turning to Washington, Senator Watson, Democrat of Mississippi, and head of the powerful—"

Pam turned it off. They looked at one another. After consideration, Jerry said, "Ouch!"

"Yes," Pam said. "'However.' Ouch indeed. Can we sue or anything? 'Asserts,' indeed!"

"No," Jerry said. "They're much too careful. They—"

"*Jerry!*" Pam said. "The poor man. Do you suppose, while we were sitting there waiting for him, he was—*Jerry!*"

"Yes," Jerry said, "I suppose so. It's—" He stopped. Byron Kingsley was looking from one to the other of them, bewilderment—even consternation—on his handsome, friendly face.

Jerry said he was sorry. He said it was this way, and told Kingsley, briefly, the way it was.

"Wanted to see you?" Kingsley repeated. "But—why?"

"We don't know," Pam said. "If we did—"

"But when he talked to you," Kingsley said. "He didn't say what he wanted to see Mr. North about? You'd think he—" He stopped and shook his head.

Pam shook hers.

"Not even a hint?" Kingsley said and then, quickly, "I'm sorry, ma'am. It's just that it seems like—wanting to see an important man like Mr. North—he'd have—well, have—" He floundered to a stop, and, Pam thought, reddened slightly.

"I know," she said. "But, he didn't. Only, as Jerry said, that it was something important. We supposed it was something about his wife's death. Anybody'd think that. But as to what—" She shrugged slender shoulders.

Byron Kingsley looked at her intently, and nodded his head as she spoke.

"Look, ma'am," he said. "Mrs. North. I didn't mean—" Once more he stopped.

"Of course not," Pam said. "It was a perfectly natural thing to—to wonder about."

"If he knew something," Kingsley said, a little as if he were speaking to himself, "about Miss Towne's death, I mean, why would he want to tell you about it—you and Mr. North? Instead of the police?"

"I don't know," Jerry said. "I suppose, because her body was found in our suite. That telephone call she got while you were there. Are you sure she said something like 'Judd.' Or, more likely, 'Judge'?"

"Pretty sure."

"It couldn't have been, say, 'Russ'? I suppose people called him that."

"You mean, he was the one who was coming? And—maybe saw something? Ran into—somebody? There?"

Jerry nodded his head.

Kingsley put long, sensitive fingers to his forehead, in an attitude of thought.

"I just barely heard the last," he said, and spoke slowly. "I told you what I thought it sounded like. But—it might have been something else. I suppose it might have been 'Russ.'"

"When you were talking to her," Pam said. "She didn't say anything about her husband. About Mr. Barnes?"

"No. I thought she was a maiden lady. Calling herself 'Miss' the way she did. Anyway, she just asked things about me, and I answered as well as I could. I thought she was mighty nice."

"Somebody didn't," Jerry said.

Kingsley put his glass down and stood up. He said he hadn't meant to make a visit of it. Jerry stood too.

"That man who worked for her," Kingsley said. "You ever run across him? Gray? Tony Gray, he calls himself?"

Jerry shook his head. Then he said, "Oh, the man who interviewed you first? The preliminary interview?"

"Yes," Kingsley said. "Young chap—works for the company. The network, they call it. I got a feeling he didn't like Miss Towne much. It wasn't anything he said, particularly, but—you know how you get feelings about that sort of thing?"

"Yes."

"Only one thing," Kingsley said. "When he left I said I'd probably be seeing him. The way one does, not knowing whether it's true. And he said, 'That's up to the fair lady, my friend.' And then something like, 'About the fair lady you can't tell. None of us can. Any day I may be out on my ear.'" He looked at Pam. "Only," he said, "he didn't say 'ear' exactly."

He was really sweet, Pam thought. Naïve, but sweet. She tried to look like a belle of the Old South, who probably couldn't ever—no, evah—guess what Mr. Gray could possibly have said. Not *evah*.

They went back toward the door, though the devastated living room. Martini was curled on top of the painters' midden—curled, it seemed, precariously, on paint-crusted canvas. It was an odd place for a cat to sleep except, of course, to a cat.

Martini opened large blue eyes and then, apparently on seeing Byron Kingsley, narrowed them again and laid her ears back. Then she leaped from the canvas and went away with speed, skirting Kingsley rather, Pam thought, offensively. There could be no doubt that having painters made Martini very nervous. As, Pam thought further, saying goodnight to Jerry's so profitable author, it does me.

***

They did not know where Judge Roger Parkman had gone. The butler had said that; Mrs. Parkman, when Mullins had got to her—after some little persuasion—had said that.

"Gone away for a few days," Mullins reported to Bill Weigand, at West Twentieth Street, at a little after eleven at night. "Don't know where. Didn't ask where. We buy that, loot?"

The question was rhetorical. They didn't buy it, and Sergeant Mullins knew they didn't buy it. It was not so clear, however, what they did do with it.

"A man's wife asks," Mullins said. "If he don't say, she asks again. Until he says. Something, anyway. Judge or no judge."

"Right," Bill said. "Some time around eight, they said? Just before you got there?"

That was what they had said. They—the butler first when Sergeant Mullins rang the doorbell of the Parkmans' house on the Upper East Side—had said it several times. Judge Parkman had gone out a few minutes before Mullins arrived, and he would be gone several days, and it was not known where he could be reached.

He had taken a suitcase with him; he had packed the suitcase himself. He had told his wife only that it was a matter of business, but had not described the business or indicated where it was to be conducted.

"You didn't ask him?" Mullins asked Mrs. Parkman, and made no effort to mask incredulity.

"Certainly not," she had told him. She was in her sixties; she was stiffly corseted and had carefully arranged graying hair. "If the judge had thought it important for me to know, he would have told me, sergeant."

Would she know what clothes he had taken? What kind of clothes, for example? Mullins had been patient. If the judge were going to a city—Chicago, say—he would take business clothes. But if he were going some place for a few days' rest—the Greenbrier, say. Or Florida, say—he would probably take the kind of clothes people wore there. Informal clothes. Perhaps a summer-weight suit, if he planned on Florida. Perhaps golf clothes. And clubs, for that matter. Did Mrs. Parkman know?

"Certainly not," she said. (But she made it sound rather as if Judge Parkman might, for all she knew, have been carrying golf clubs in his pocket.) Her tone had implied that the question was stupid, possibly crass. As if, her tone said, such commonplace matters were any concern of hers!

"Lying?" Weigand said.

"Sure," Mullins said. "Very high-toned lady. Lying, and not even trying to make it sound good."

"A powder?"

"Sure he took a powder. Only thing is, why? To let this stink—this business about what he said on TV—die down? Or?"

"Right," Bill said. "We know a lot of good questions, as always. Any good answers, Mullins?"

Mullins had not. He said, "On the teletyper?"

"Not yet," Weigand told him. "We'll ask around a bit first. Right?"

"O.K., loot," Mullins said, knowing who would ask around.

VII

It is not difficult to compile a statistical summary of a life—not when there are enough men to look through enough records, carry on enough interviews, in a sufficient number of places. At a little after eight o'clock Friday morning, the fifteenth of November, Weigand had the measurements of a life in front of him on his desk. The life had been so long; marked by such and such events. It had been lived by a woman five feet six inches tall, weighing one hundred and twenty-two pounds, having blond hair (rinsed) and blue eyes and teeth which had been beautifully recapped for symmetry; a woman who had died of asphyxia resulting from smothering (presumably homicidal, presumably by a pillow). Weigand could, from the information in front of him, have written a biography of Amanda Towne—if he had known anything of any real importance about her.

The things of no real importance had, of course, to be known, and so had been found out. Born, Hot Springs, Arkansas, September 10, 1913. (Daughter of Mr. and Mrs. Vincent Towne; second of two children; brother, Vincent Towne, Jr., now living in Seattle. Contact made.) B.A. from the University of Arkansas, 1934. Briefly employed on a Memphis newspaper—June to October, 1934. On staff of the Chicago *Press-Bulletin*, November, 1934, to August, 1942. Married to Russell Barnes, reporter and war correspondent, February 28, 1936. No record of divorce. Transferred to New York by Continental Broadcasting Corporation in 1946. Radio show expanded to an hour; given title "People Next Door." (Title owned by the corporation.) Show switched to television in 1951, but heard also on radio until early 1953. Residence since 1953, Hotel Breckenridge.

All very interesting, possibly in the end all very important. But who was she? What was she like? Why, now, was she dead? There were no convenient statistics to cover such matters. Oh yes—died,

November 13 of the current year, probably between seven and eight P.M.

She had gone about a good deal, with a good many people—she had attended parties, and given parties, and gone to theaters and eaten at restaurants—at the Algonquin, at Sardi's, at "21." (And probably at Automats, and at drugstore lunch counters, and at restaurants in the country.) She had owned a Chrysler Imperial, 1957. (Hardtop.) In 1956, she had rented a house in Westport.

Other things remained to be found out. She had had men friends, presumably—she had been a reasonably young and very pretty woman, and she and her husband had been separated for years. (Why? For how many years? With what kind of relationship remaining between them?) If there had been one man closer than others, that did not yet appear. It would be found out; such things are not often hidden.

She had a business manager named Alice Fleming, and an agent named Orson Bart. She had recently signed a new two-year contract with CBC. It was to be presumed that her brother in Seattle would inherit what money she left, which it was to be presumed might be a good deal. (Unless she had been less prudent as a business woman than anything in the statistics—including the figures on her new contract—indicated.)

All he needed to know to write a biography, Bill Weigand thought—all except a woman to put into it. Things about a woman—obviously. Many and more to come. The woman herself? A wax figure in a store window, brightly lighted now, no more than that as yet.

Seattle had been asked to help; Hot Springs was checking back; in Chicago men made additional enquiries. Mullins and Detective Frankel, teamed for the time, asked discreetly about one of the men whose life hers had touched. Detective Hanson would check out on the Norths and Bleeck's. (Which was a waste of Detective Hanson's time and abilities.) Three men worked patiently at the Hotel Breckenridge. A Mr. Lovelace, who had been the previous occupant of the Norths' suite—and who might have carried a key off with him, and come back to use it, or given it to somebody to use—would be interviewed in Galveston, when he got there. He appeared to have stopped off somewhere. . . .

Alice Fleming was not at the Continental Broadcasting Corporation's building on Madison Avenue—a building, Weigand thought absently, somehow too substantial to be held up only by words, by light patterns. (Which was manifestly absurd.) Her address would be provided. A man named Tony Gray, who had worked with Amanda Towne for the past year, interviewing guests for her, would not be in until six in the evening, when he would be one of several who got the late news reports together. Who else would Captain Weigand like to talk to?

"Anybody who knew her well," Bill Weigand told the young-old man at the wide desk; the man in the narrow suit. "Did you?"

"Businesswise," the young-old man said.

"Characterwise?" Bill said, gravely. The young-old man grinned, and looked younger.

"No," he said. "Fact is, I just switched over from CBS. Oh—I knew a lot about her. Everybody on the street knows a lot about 'Mandy' Towne. Ratingwise—" He paused. Then he said, "Hell, why not? As good as most words. Ratingwise she was terrific. For an afternoon slot."

"I know a good deal about her," Weigand said. "Who knew *her*?"

That required telephone conferences—most of which wandered into other fields, and tended to remain there. Bill was patient.

"Jimmy Fergus knew her in Chicago," the young-old man said. "Old voice of doom." A telephone rang and he listened and said, "O.K. Be right along," and hung up. "Came east with her," he said. "She brought him along, as a matter of fact. He might be your man." He looked at his watch. "On the air now," he said. "Eleven o'clock newscast. You can catch him down on the eighth floor."

Weigand went down from the twelfth floor to the eighth. "Studio G," a girl with copper hair told him. "Down that way." He went down that way, along a corridor through which many moved, for the most part at high speed. A sign glowed red at the door of Studio G. It said, "On The Air." Bill waited. After a few minutes the sign went off. He went into Studio G, which was small and hushed. A gray-haired man in his sixties sat at a small table, behind a microphone. He supported a heavy head in his hands. He looked up and Bill Weigand said, "Mr. Fergus?"

The man nodded his head, without removing it from his hands.

"The Middle East gets me," he said, morosely.

"It seems to get everybody," Bill said.

The heavy gray-haired man took his hands down and looked at them and said, "Oh. That. I suppose so. It's those damned names. French names, German names, Italian names—now Arabs. You're a new one, aren't you?"

"I—" Bill began.

"Producer?" James Fergus said. "Assistant producer? Director? Assistant director? Or—a vice president?"

Bill told him who he was, and what he had come about.

"A great girl," Fergus said. "Wonderful. They won't find another one like Mandy. This Casey girl they're talking about. Not that the Casey girl isn't good. But ratingwise—"

"Casey girl?"

"To take over the show. Maureen Casey. Been doing five-minute breaks for—what difference does it make? She's all right. Not Mandy but— What do you want to know about Mandy?"

The answer was "Everything." Weigand did not make it. He said, "Whatever you can tell me."

"Nothing that'll help," Fergus said. "However—you feel it is too early for a drink?"

For the first time, Weigand thought, he spoke like an announcer. Possibly because he spoke of an important matter.

It was too early for a drink, at eleven-thirty. Much too early.

But detectives cannot be slaves of habits, even of the best of habits.

"Right," Bill said. "If you like."

Fergus liked. In a small restaurant off Madison—where a surprising number did not, it seemed, feel eleven-thirty too early for a drink—they sat at a corner table, and Fergus drank bourbon on the rocks. He drank thirstily; said he needed that. Then he said, "I don't mind telling you, it's knocked me. Mandy. And then poor old Russ." He drank again. "Poor old Russ. Poor old Carl. Poor old— The hell with it." He raised his glass, and a waiter saw it. The waiter knew what to do about it—from experience, Bill Weigand assumed. The waiter looked at Weigand's almost untouched martini glass. Weigand shook his head.

"Last time I saw her," Fergus said, "after the show Wednesday. No different from any time—keyed up, like she always was. Wouldn't have been any good if she didn't get keyed up. Jumped Tony because a woman she interviewed froze on the air. Thought he should have tipped her off. Scratchy with the Fleming a little, but the Fleming's used to it. Said I made everything sound like a funeral."

"This was unusual?"

"I just said— Good. I can use that." The waiter had brought another drink. "I just said, standard order of procedure. She got keyed up. She got unwound. On top of the world when she left."

"She was—difficult?"

"No more than most. Less than most. Look, I can't tell you anything that's any good. Saw her three times a week, read what they gave me to read."

"I gathered," Bill said, "that you knew her well. Had known her for a long time."

"Twenty years ago," Fergus said. "You can call that a long time. Yes. You can call that a long time. But, what's it got to do with—what you want? With who killed her?"

Bill didn't know. He said the obvious—the obvious that always needed saying. He did not know what anything had to do with it. He said, "You knew Barnes? I gather you did."

"In the old days," Fergus said. "Oh, ran into him now and then these days. Nothing to talk about any more."

"Did Miss Towne see much of him?"

Fergus drank. He shrugged heavy shoulders. He said, "How would I know?" and then, "I shouldn't suppose so. Who was poor old Russ?"

"Her husband. She gets killed. He gets killed."

"Not working at it," Fergus said. "I don't know why either of them got killed. Why would I?"

"Listen," Bill said, and thought, from the effect of a swallow of a second drink, that James Fergus might have had a first, at least, even before eleven-thirty. "Listen, Mr. Fergus. All I'm trying to find out is what sort of person Amanda Towne was. It may explain something."

"People get killed because of the kind of people they are?"

"Sometimes."

"Maybe. In the old days, it was because they got out of line. What kind of woman was Mandy? Bright as they come. Ambitious. Had whatever it is it takes. Voice. Looks. Get people talking and keep them talking. Always could do that. What's the matter with your drink?"

"Nothing," Bill said, and sipped to prove it. "Would she have found out something and passed it on to Barnes? Asked him to check into it further?"

"What?"

"Obviously," Bill said, "I don't know."

"Why would she? If she wanted something checked into, what would be the matter with Tony Gray? That's what they pay him for."

"I don't know," Bill said. "Is that what they pay Gray for?"

"He's what they call a writer," Fergus said. "What *they* call a writer. On Mandy's show he went around and talked to people press agents wanted to get on. Made notes. Passed them along to Mandy. Worked out a rough script. Not that she used a script. The rest of the time, he's one of the guys who watches the news tickers. Roughs out five, fifteen minutes of newscast—whatever the period is—hands it along to Ben or somebody to rewrite. Then it comes along to me, or somebody, to read."

"What'll he do now? Now that Miss Towne's dead. Work for —what's her name—Miss Casey?"

"I don't know. Take a vice president to decide an important thing like that. More damn vice presidents."

"And you? Will you announce for Miss Casey? If she does take over the show?"

"Doesn't look like it," Fergus said. "Nobody's passed the word."

"Who is Carl?"

"Carl? What about Carl?"

"I don't know," Bill said. "You mentioned somebody named Carl. Poor old Carl. Poor old Russ."

"And poor old Fergus. Whyn't you finish it? The middle-aged musketeers, one for all and all for Mandy. Till death do us part. Carl Cunningham. The one who was going to set the world on fire. Dead, for all I know. Like Russ. Like our fair lady." He finished his drink. "Or," he said, "did you think they made that up for the play? Called her that twenty years ago."

Weigand nodded, and lighted a cigarette and sipped his drink. And waited.

"More than twenty years ago," Fergus said. "Twenty-five, almost. A quarter of a century. Longer when you think of it that way, isn't it?" Bill nodded his head. "I was city editor," Fergus said. "Going places. We were all going places. You know how it is? I was going places and Russ was going places and poor old Carl. And along comes our fair lady."

It was not especially clear. It merited an encouraging "um-mm," and got one.

"Not that she did anything," Fergus said. "Except—" He paused, and finished his drink and looked at the empty glass. "Guess not," he said to the glass. "Got to be sober by two. Friday—" He stopped again. "Keep forgetting," he said. "No more Mandy. No more people next door. The hell—" He lifted his glass and the waiter saw it, and went toward the bar. "You know how a light bulb burns out?"

Weigand by no means followed. He merely waited.

"Burning along even and steady when you turn it off one night," he said. "Turn it on the next day and the poor old filaments can't take it. See what I mean? Too much current for the poor old filaments. Just an instant first—brighter than it ever was, then. You know? Dazzle you, it's so bright. And then—phut. And you screw another bulb in and so what?"

The waiter brought another drink. But Fergus merely nodded, to show he saw, and did not reach for it.

"City editor," Fergus said. "Told you that, didn't I? And Russ was the top man on the staff, and he'd been a war correspondent when he wasn't much more than a kid and Carl was our Washington man, lambasting the hell out of Roosevelt. The old man didn't like Roosevelt. Carl did, but what the hell? He worked there. Some of the stories he sent along—wow! All of us going places, we thought. Getting along in the forties, all three of us. Funny thing about the forties." He stopped and looked at Weigand.

"Is it?" Bill said. "What, Mr. Fergus?"

"Better than you've ever been before," Fergus said. "And—what next? Maybe you get still better—maybe I get to be managing editor. Executive editor. Maybe—maybe not. But, you don't stay right there. You know it by then. Every now and then you think about it. But you say, What the hell? Another day coming. And then you say, I'll never be any better than I am right now and if I'm going to break out of it, now's the time." Suddenly, unexpectedly, he smiled. The smile lighted his face. It went out—like a light bulb burned out. "About then," Fergus said, "a lot of newspapermen go into publicity. On the idea of making it while the making's good." He drank, but not thirstily. "Not," he said, "that there was so much to make in the 'thirties."

"About Miss Towne?" Weigand said. "And the rest of you? This—Carl, you say?"

"Carl Cunningham," Fergus said. "About Mandy. Maybe she

was the extra current. That the poor old filaments couldn't take. Or—the air blast from a bellows on a log that's just glowing along, minding its own business. And then flares up. And burns out. Only—not at first."

At first, Amanda Towne was a girl from a small-town paper, looking for a job on a big-town paper—pretty, but not much prettier than others; bright, but not so bright as all that. A girl who talked like Arkansas, and wore new clothes she had bought in Chicago, and who sat in the applicant's not especially comfortable chair at the end of a city editor's desk in November of 1934 and said she wanted a job. At a time when they were not taking any new people on. A girl who sat through interruptions—telephones ringing, the "got-a-new-lead-coming-up-Jim," the "here's-the-dummy-for-the-makeover-Jim."

And all the time, James Fergus, in his forties and going places, could feel her there. It was as if she gave off heat. Not that that was right; that it was anything he could then (or could now) put a word to, a word that was adequate, that explained. It was not because she was a pretty girl; pretty girls were no novelty to James Fergus in those days, or to Carl Cunningham or Russell Barnes. You took pretty girls, when available, or left them alone. Not that that did not enter into it, but that was later. At first—

"If I had to explain it now," James Fergus, in his sixties, having a drink he didn't need too early in the day, "I'd say she was radio-active. That we were Geiger counters and when she was around we clicked faster and faster. We, and a lot of others. Men *and* women. But mostly Carl and Russ and me."

That was after, for no reason of real need, James Fergus, city editor, had told a girl from Arkansas (with only small-city experience, and not much of that) that they'd give her a try on the Chicago *Press-Bulletin*. It was some time after.

"Oh," Fergus told Bill Weigand, "she turned out to be good at the job. Wrote 'em too long at first, as kids do—every story the greatest story ever. Too long, and she choked up sometimes. Most of them do, particularly most girls. But she got good fast and, boy, could she interview! People who said 'no comment' to everybody else would talk their heads off for her—and, plenty of times, say a lot of things they wished afterward they hadn't said. But there wasn't ever any real come-back on any of her stuff. Now and then somebody'd feel he'd been taken advantage of somehow, but he never knew quite how and couldn't ever prove anything. I don't know that I ever saw anybody get to be a pro so fast. But it wasn't that."

He was silent at the table across from Bill Weigand for what seemed a long time. "I keep saying what it wasn't about her," he said, then. "Not what it was, because I don't know what it was. All I know is, it got all of us and made us—dissatisfied. I guess that's it. Made us feel—dull, as if we were half alive. Perhaps that's what I'm trying to say about her. She was more alive than anybody else. In those days, anyway. What good's this to you? It was a quarter of a century ago. Not the Mandy who—who died the other night. A long time after the rest of us had."

"I want," Bill said, "to find out what she was like. What she was all about. I told you that."

The bond between the four of them—the middle-aged "musketeers" and the "fair lady"—had grown slowly. Carl Cunningham came back from Washington in the spring after Amanda Towne was hired on the *Press-Bulletin* staff. By that time, Fergus and Barnes and the girl were much together—having lunch together, sometimes having long dinners—and long talk—and walking to nowhere in particular on spring evenings. Cunningham became one of the group, made it a group of four.

It was only that for the first year, and no competition for Amanda. "Actually, there never got to be." And not, at first, any "dissatisfaction." The men were older—Cunningham, the youngest of them, was twenty years older than Amanda Towne—and there was a good deal in it of telling a child how a trade ran, and how the world ran. "Remember," Fergus said, "we were all pretty good at the trade. Then."

More like uncles they were, that first summer—that summer of 1935. Uncles showing a pretty niece a city, telling her about a trade. Not always all of them together. Not all of them were often free together. And there were other things, other girls. And there was, then, no jealousy, no competition. Fergus repeated that. No competition, at any rate, of the usual kind—one girl and three men after her. They had not been after her—not then, not in that sense. It had been easy that first summer, when it was she who was learning, and no uneasiness about themselves had developed yet. It had been companionable and relaxed, and had meant nothing except what each moment of it meant.

The change had come gradually; there was no easy way to put a finger on the moment the change had come—to hold an instant between thumb and forefinger and show it and say, "This was it. This was when it changed." It was a long time ago; and the change had been subtle.

"We were talking mostly about her," James Fergus told Weigand, at a table, in a little restaurant off Madison. "About—oh, where she had been, where she was going, how to get there. 'This is the way you do it, my girl'—that was what it came to. Then—we were telling her about ourselves. Where we had been. Where we were going. And—where were we going? That was it. Carl and I were having a drink some place—it must have been sometime in the fall. The fall of 'thirty-five, I guess. Waiting for her—for Russ. Carl—"

Carl Cunningham was a tall man; a tall, thin man with black hair, which often needed pushing back, and black eyes. He had moments when, suddenly, he was abrupt. He set his glass down on the bar harder than he needed to. He turned, leaning down a little on the bar, and looked at Fergus and said, "Where's it getting us, Jim?"

Once Jim Fergus had discovered that "it" was indeterminate: that "it" meant everything—the question seemed only one of those things men say when there is a sudden darkness over the mind, and usually when they have been drinking for some time. But Carl Cunningham had not been drinking for any time at all; he seldom drank much. "We're not getting any younger," Carl said, and that, too, was the worn remark everybody makes, when the shadow crosses the mind. "So what the hell?" Fergus said, which was another of the worn things to say. "Who is?" Fergus said. "Even our fair lady—"

"What's she got to do with it?" Carl Cunningham said—and said it so quickly, with such abruptness, that for the first time Fergus knew the girl did have something to do with it. He had said, "Finish your drink, Carl. Don't cry into it." Carl started, Fergus thought, to get angry, but instead grinned and said, "The old reliable. Always trust good old Jim." Then he stared at his drink and said, suddenly, "Maybe she has, at that. She's—she's so damned young. It's—disturbing to—" He let it trail off, gave up trying to phrase it. "One of these days," he said, "I'm going to get out of this rat race and set up shop."

"Half of them," Fergus told Bill Weigand, "were always going to 'set up shop.' Chuck the business, write what they wanted to. Novels and stories, mostly. It never hit me. I was always on the other side. Desk man. Telling others what to write. But—Carl was one of them. Mostly, nothing comes of it. But the next spring—"

There was no reason, by the next spring, that James Fergus should have been surprised when Carl Cunningham quit his job—although he was offered more money to stay on, and in the 'thirties there were few offers of more money. Fergus was feeling it himself, by then—feeling the restlessness, the uneasiness; feeling that if he was ever going to get anywhere he had better be about it. But he was surprised, all the same. And Russell Barnes was surprised.

Amanda Towne wasn't. One could tell she wasn't. She nodded, as if she had known all along that this would happen. She said that it was Carl's life, and that probably he was right, and she said, "He's different from the rest of us."

Neither of the men had noticed that, particularly. Or thought, at any rate, more of it than that men differ from one another. The three of them were having lunch, and Carl had been gone a week—gone back to Arkansas, where he had come from, and found some out-of-the-way place to live, where living wouldn't cost too much—had, in short, set up shop.

"He's talked to me a lot about a novel he wants to write," she told them, seeing lack of comprehension in their faces. "It might be—might be something. Anyway, I think it might."

"I suppose," Fergus told Bill Weigand across the table, "all she'd done was listen. She could always listen—listen in a way that made you feel you had something special to say, were saying something special. That's what always made her such a good interviewer, of course. There was something—something positive about the way she listened. She'd listened to Carl, I suppose—listened and been young, and made him feel young—young and ready for anything."

Fergus was drinking very slowly, now. He seemed half at the table, half in the Chicago of almost a quarter of a century before.

"Made him think he was more than he was, had more than he had," Fergus said. "At least, it seems to have turned out that way. I watched magazines and book announcements for a year or two—he quit writing back after the first few weeks—and I never saw any deathless prose by Carl. Poor old Carl. Tried to live up to that 'difference' she saw in him and—well, there you are."

"You think she wanted that?"

Fergus said, "Hell no." He didn't blame the girl. Not about Carl or anything else. He didn't suppose Carl did. It was just one of those things.

"He was in love with her?"

"Maybe. It didn't show. I did gather—maybe from something she said later—that he had asked her to go with him and she'd said no, or not then, or something. Anyway, she married Russ the next fall. I was off the sheet by then. Going on to bigger and better things. She'd been listening to me, by then."

Only that—listening, saying perhaps he was right, saying that she supposed newspaper work did, often, come slow and tedious circle, back to the rim of a copy desk—or to supervision of the clipping files, the "morgue."

"The poor old guy who ran the morgue had been a managing editor in his time," Fergus told Weigand. "We had a couple more, and a chief correspondent for Europe, the whole damn continent, on our rim. But everybody knows that when he gets into it. Only—"

Only, that summer—the summer of 1936—he had got an offer from the Continental Broadcasting Corporation. It was the first such offer he had got—offers of jobs which paid better, had potentially brighter futures. Maybe he had finally got around to being ready. Maybe—maybe it was the same way it had been with Carl Cunningham. "Being listened to. Getting—stimulated."

The job was assistant chief of the news department for Continental, in the Chicago area. It paid three times what he had been getting. He had just taken the job over when Barnes and Amanda Towne got married. That had surprised him, too. And—

"No," he said, in answer to a question Bill Weigand had not asked. "I wasn't in love with her. As a matter of fact, I was having a round with—" He shrugged. "No," he said again. "Anyway, I don't think so. Didn't think so then. They only lasted about a year."

"They?"

"Mandy and poor old Russ. She was—I guess she was too much for him. Too young. I don't mean the obvious thing, although that might have been part of it. I mean just—well, living in a world full of expectancy. Trying to keep up. Trying too hard. He left the sheet after they split up and—he wasn't ever as good again. Oh, he was all right. He had a lot of jobs before this last one. But—the momentum wasn't there any more. You know what I mean?"

"You don't know what happened to Cunningham?"

"No."

"To yourself?"

"You can see, can't you? Oh, there are always shuffles going on in the business. This one up and that one down, when somebody gets a bright idea. Not out—just somewhere else. Not as good as the place you were before. At least, it was that way with me. I got her her first radio job while I still had what it took—part time, news of interest to women. That was around 'thirty-eight, 'thirty-nine. She stayed on the paper for two or three years and then CBC made her a real offer. Contract and a half-hour spot. Not me—I'd been shuffled a bit by then. But I did get her her start."

"She appreciated that?"

"Yes. Mentioned it every now and then. Brought me along east when they moved her east. The Chicago office figured they could get along without me."

"Now?"

"What do you mean, now?"

"Her—not being around. Will it affect you?"

"It might. But no, I doubt it. Maybe it will even work out better—not so much pressure. She'd—got a little hard to please, our fair lady had, the last few years. Kept trying to get what she called a lift in it. Thought I didn't have this lift. As God knows I haven't, any more. But now—now I imagine things will just jog along for a while. Five minutes newscast here, fifteen minutes there. Where it doesn't matter too much. Nobody to make a point of 'lift.' "

"If she had been—really dissatisfied with you? Made an issue of it?"

"That could have been just too bad," Fergus said, and then suddenly set his glass down hard. "What are you trying to prove?"

"Nothing," Bill said. "Just the picture. The drinks are on me, Mr. Fergus."

"The hell they are," Fergus said. "After that crack—the hell they are, captain."

VIII

AT FIVE-THIRTY Friday evening, Bill Weigand rang the Norths' apartment and got no answer. He had rung it an hour earlier, and got a man with an Italian accent, who had said, "Nobodya here, mister," and hung up. It had been, on the whole, a frustrating afternoon—an afternoon of chaff and very little wheat. Such afternoons are to be expected, but need not be welcomed.

Mullins had not found Judge Parkman. He had talked to a good many people who might be expected to know where Judge Parkman might have gone. None of them had known. Mrs. Parkman declined to see Mullins, or to explain why she would not. So, if the ruffled judge had been the visitor Amanda Towne expected—or had planned to meet—he could not be given the opportunity to insist that (a) he had never been near the place or Miss Towne or (b) that he had been there, and she was fine—just fine—when he left. So, frustration, presumably temporary.

Seattle had not yet helped. Hot Springs was still checking back. Chicago had added additional information, which tallied with the information Weigand already had—with the supplementary report that James Fergus had been on the losing side of a minor civil war at CBC in the late 'thirties, and that was what had happened to James Fergus. Mr. Lovelace, who might have walked off with a key to the Norths' suite at the Breckenridge, still tarried short of Galveston. A waiter at Bleeck's remembered that a couple answering the description of Mr. and Mrs. Gerald North had indeed arrived at the restaurant around five o'clock the previous afternoon, and had ordered—and drunk—martinis. And had eventually been joined by a man answering the description of Captain William Weigand of Homicide, Manhattan West. Which was nice to know.

Jerry's author, Mr. Byron Kingsley, who had admittedly talked to Amanda Towne shortly before her death, and who coincidentally came from Arkansas—which made three of them —was not at his hotel. He would be given a message asking him to call Captain Weigand at his convenience.

Tony Gray breakfasted at one o'clock in the afternoon in a small apartment in the Murray Hill area. He had known Amanda Towne for a year or so; he worked for the network, and was assigned to her show, as a "legman." Which meant that he found out whether people who offered themselves as "People Next Door," or were offered by others, would be likely to have anything to say, and to be able to say it.

"Ad lib, you know," Gray told Weigand, who accepted a cup of coffee. "Some of them talk an arm off. Others freeze—like this poor old dame Wednesday. This Grandmother of the Year. God."

Amanda had been a very smooth operator. He had never seen a better. "Not even Mary Margaret." You couldn't ask for a better person to work with than Amanda Towne. Wonderful woman, altogether, and it was hard to believe that anybody would do a thing like that to her. Everybody loved her; everybody he'd run into, anyway. (Her estranged husband was not, it appeared, among the people he had run into.) He had heard that James Fergus had once held a much different, and much more important, job with the network and that, only a few years ago, he had been M.C. on a couple of pretty good shows. Of course, Fergus was getting along. Voice showed it. You couldn't hide it in the voice.

Tony Gray was quick and red haired and in his twenties—a young man going places. The next week, as a matter of fact, he and a photographer were going to Singapore for a picture job. He wouldn't, then, act as a legman for whoever took over "People Next Door"?

Not he. As a matter of fact, they wouldn't have kept him on that job—which was interesting, but didn't lead places—if Mandy hadn't insisted. Now that she could no longer insist—

He slowed down a little at that point. Not, he said, that he wouldn't have been damned glad to work with her as long as she wanted. Still—

"Right," Bill said, and went to talk to Alice Fleming, who was heavy and black haired, and had an office—a small office—on Fifth Avenue and who said that Amanda Towne had been a fine person to work with, if you knew how to handle her—they all took handling, the ones in her line—and if you kept your end up.

Alice Fleming had known Amanda Towne since Amanda came on from Chicago; she had been her business manager for five years or so. And, to be honest, Amanda had needed a business manager. Otherwise, she would have spent everything she had. Poured it down the drain. If she and Orson Bart—"He was her agent, you know"—had not kept an eye on things—well! "For an example, there was this man down in Arkansas—somebody she used to work with. In Chicago, I think. Trying to be a writer, he was, and not making it. She sent him a check every month until Bart and I took over, and why? What did it get her?"

"A man named Cunningham?" Bill said, offering no theory as to what generosity might have got Amanda Towne.

"Heard about him, have you? From poor old Jim?"

"Right," Bill said. "She'd stopped sending him money?"

"Unless she squeezed it out of what we let her keep. I wouldn't put it past her—helping lame dogs over stiles. That was Mandy. A great girl, but—" She stopped at that, and looked at Weigand intently from shrewd black eyes. He was not, she told him, to get any ideas about her and Bart. All they got was their percentages, if he was getting notions. The rest went to a fund. So that Amanda Towne would have something when—when, Bill supposed, her voice got old.

Alice Fleming had no idea who would do a thing like that to Mandy, or want to. Unless it was one of the nuts she had interviewed. A lot of them were nuts. This Judge What's-his-name, for example. He had really been fussed, and blamed it on Mandy. Instead of on his own big mouth. Perhaps, among the hundreds of people who had been through Amanda Towne's mill in the years of its grinding one might have held a grudge.

Perhaps—perhaps— But, actually, she hadn't the foggiest, although she certainly wished the police luck.

"She hadn't," Bill said, "had any changes in mind? On the show?"

"Changes? What do you mean, changes?"

Bill didn't know what he meant. If he knew, he would not need to ask. Personnel changes, perhaps? Changes in format which might, in some fashion, affect personnel.

"You mean poor old Jim?"

He meant nothing specific. He was looking for something specific. What about Mr. Fergus?

"She thought he was a drag on the show," Alice Fleming said. "She'd planned to ask them to put another announcer on. For the good of the show. That's the only thing I know about."

"If she'd asked that," Bill said, "they'd have done what she asked?"

He was damn right. At least that much. It could be that—

She stopped. He waited.

"All right," she said, "poor old Jim's getting on. He's got a lot of chores around CBC—commercials, newscasts, weather reports. But, if Mandy had made a pitch they might have taken another look at him. You see what I mean? Thought, maybe the girl's right. Maybe he *is* a drag on things. Maybe—" She shrugged. "I don't know," she said. "I don't work for CBC. Probably he'd just have gone on with his other chores."

In other words, Bill thought now—sitting at his desk, reaching for a report in the "In" basket—Fergus might have been fired entirely. Would he kill to keep his job? And kill another man, too—killing him by brute strength, and brutally? If so, why?

Plenty of questions, as always. Had Alice Fleming been too quick to deny an imputation not made—the imputation that she and a man named Bart had been up to funny business with the money Amanda Towne made? Another question, another thing to be checked out.

The "In" report was from Detective (first grade) Freddy Willings, who had been the one sent to see what could be found out at the Hotel Breckenridge because it was in hotels like the Breckenridge he had grown up.

They had spent most of the day going over the suite which Amanda Towne had occupied—occupied for several years, so that her personality had impinged, so that its atmosphere was no longer heavy with the hotel's stately neutrality. (Some of the furniture, for example, was hers; all the pictures were hers.) It was a suite of living room (twenty-five feet by fifteen) and a bedroom; a dressing room off a bath; a serving pantry, which was in effect a small, neat kitchen. (Sketch of suite enclosed.) There were twin beds, each of full bed size, in the bedroom. There were two sofas and four upholstered chairs (two of modern design) in the living room. There were a great many clothes in two large closets. They included a mink coat, a mink stole and a sealskin coat. There was a desk, with letters and checkbooks and memoranda, and such other things as accumulate in a busy person's desk. (All duly gathered up, labeled, and forwarded for further inspection.) There were a great many fingerprints—Amanda's own, those of her personal maid (see report subjoined), some of hotel maids, and some which were merely fingerprints at large. These last had been sent through the machine—and the machine had been momentarily pleased, if a little surprised, to find that one had been made by J. L. Roscoe (alias a good many other things) who had left a rather fascinating trail of forged checks from one end of the country to the other before the Federal Bureau of Investigation caught up with him.

(The machine's pleasure in this identification was sharply diminished when a question or two revealed that Mr. Roscoe had been on "People Next Door" a week earlier and had talked interestingly about the methods of check forgers and countermeasures of circumvention.)

They had found two glasses on a coffee table, and that neither of them had contained anything noxious. Bourbon and water had been in one, and the other, on which Miss Towne's prints were plain, had held scotch. The prints on the other glass had been those of Byron Kingsley, who had obligingly, if unconsciously, recorded them anew when he signed his statement at West Twentieth Street. This did not, apparently, advance the matter, since Kingsley had already admitted his presence. He had not, to be sure, mentioned bourbon.

There were no signs in the apartment of violence of any kind—nothing to confirm or refute the always evident possibility that she had been killed, as it were, at home and transported down the hall to Suite 718, occupied so briefly by Mr. and Mrs. Gerald North.

There were loose pillows on both sofas, and there was no mark—of, say, rouged lips—on any. But—two of the pillows were red, and red on red is not always visible to the eye. Freddy Willings had had these sent to the lab. He was a thorough man, Freddy Willings, a characteristic of which Bill Weigand highly approved. Probably, Amanda Towne had been killed where she was found (which raised more questions than it answered), but there was no harm in making sure, if that proved possible. Bill read on.

Anita Baker, personal maid, had been tracked to Harlem, and was pretty and bright and entirely co-operative. From Tuesday through Saturday of each week she had, for two years and three months, gone to Miss Towne's suite at eleven each morning and left it at five each evening, and done what Miss Towne wanted done. She had gone on Wednesday, and gone home on Wednesday—and spent most of the day going over Miss Towne's clothes, pressing here and there, and tightening a hook or two, and fixing one stuck zipper, and sending two dresses and a robe to the cleaner's. There had been nothing, up to five o'clock, to mark it off from any other day. When she came in, at around four, Miss Towne had been as she usually was about four—a little tired, a little let down, a little in need of a cup of tea.

"Tea?" the detective repeated.

Really tea—it was always tea, at that hour. Not that, at other hours, Miss Towne had not behaved more—normally. But, when she first came home, always tea—a Lapsang souchong, brewed in pot, the time of steeping immutable. The detective wrote down the name of the tea, wondering why. Miss Towne had not said that she expected anyone to call later, or that she did not. However, she almost never mentioned her plans unless she was having several people in and wanted Anita to stay and help out.

It took Detective (third grade) Wilson a little over two hours to make the trip to Harlem, wait for Miss Anita Baker to come home from shopping, and discover that Miss Towne liked a kind of tea he had never heard of and had been no different on the last day of her life than on any other day. But the only way to find out is to ask.

Mrs. Rose Pinkney—hotel maid and cat fancier—was summoned from Brooklyn and taken more slowly, more carefully (if with somewhat less vocal vigor) over the ground Inspector O'Malley had first explored. In this instance, Detective Willings took her over it physically, took her from room to room along the corridor on the seventh floor into which opened suites 718 through 725, odd and even numbers on opposite sides.

It was established, by re-enactment in Suite 718—still vacant by police order—that Mrs. Pinkney took from eight to ten minutes to turn down beds, check towels and pick up. Willings supposed that, on less dramatized—and observed—occasions she might take a little longer. The housekeeper was watching now, an encouragement to briskness. Then, from the time she went into 718 an hour might elapse before she reached 724, which opened from the end of the corridor, being a corner suite? If, that was, she worked back and forth across the corridor? Did she?

Sometimes she did. Sometimes she worked to one side and down the other. It depended, in large measure, on how many suites she found occupied. It also depended, to some degree, on how she happened to feel at the time. "Sometimes one way, sometimes the other," she said, and added, "makes a change," and then, with a glance at the housekeeper, "no rules about it I ever heard of."

There were no rules about it. On Wednesday?

"Crisscrossed," Rose Pinkney said.

So it would have been about an hour from the time she went into Suite 718 until she reached Suite 724? Willings felt the faint stirring of a theory.

"Would have been," Rose Pinkney said. "Only I don't. Didn't, that is."

"Don't what?" Willings asked her, and was patient.

"Go in Miss Towne's suite," she said. "Not on the evening shift. On account of, it bothers her. Did, I mean. Ask her." Willings was a little startled. Mrs. Pinkney indicated the housekeeper. Willings said, "Oh."

The housekeeper said that that was true. Miss Towne had left orders, shortly after she moved into the suite, that the evening service was to be omitted. If she needed more towels, she would call for them. If she found the turning down of beds beyond her strength, she would so indicate. Meanwhile, she preferred a minimum of barging in.

"Quite often, I believe, she had conferences in her rooms," the housekeeper said. "I always assumed that she did not wish them interrupted."

"So you didn't go into her suite Wednesday?" Willings said.

"How many times—" Mrs. Pinkney began and checked it and said, "No sir."

A quarter after seven, or thereabouts, Mrs. Pinkney had gone into the suite occupied by Mr. and Mrs. North. At, say, a quarter after eight she would, then, have reached—but not entered—Suite 724, at the end of the corridor. But, since she had not entered, that now meant nothing. Miss Towne might have been still alive in the room. She might, just possibly, have been dead in the room, with the murderer still there, too, and waiting a clear coast—waiting, it could be presumed, for Mrs. Pinkney to complete her rounds and go away.

Detective Willings's theory flickered somewhat. It had been that the murderer, seeing that Mrs. Pinkney was working toward the Towne suite and having reasons to want discovery delayed—as what murderer would not?—had moved the body from a room still untended to one already visited. But, since Mrs. Pinkney did not actually go into the Towne suite, as Willings had assumed she did—

Of course. The operative word was "assumed." If he had assumed it, so might have the murderer. It was unlikely that there would, in any conversation Willings could think of, have been occasion for Miss Towne to explain that she did not like to be bothered by evening maids.

On the other hand, it was most probable that Miss Towne had been killed where found—and where a pillow was marked with red from her lips. The red—lipstick red—fabric of the loose pillows on the sofa in 724—well, it was rather interesting. It would interest those whose job it primarily was to put two and two together. Of these, Detective Willings was not yet one. So he did not incorporate his theory directly into his report, although Bill Weigand could read it between lines if he chose.

Bill Weigand did. He called the lab. They were getting around to the pillows as fast as they could. Did Bill think his was the only case in the works? Bill did not. In the morning? Sure, in the morning. Or perhaps later that night. If they found anything, they would pass on what they found. "Atta boy," Bill said, and disconnected and rang the Norths again. And was again unanswered.

He might as well, Bill decided, surprise Dorian by dropping in for dinner. And surprise, and delight, himself. He drove uptown and east, and went up to an apartment which had windows overlooking the East River—an apartment much too expensive for a police captain who did not have some money of his own (inherited too late to sustain him through law school, else he would probably not have been a police captain) and whose wife was not a reasonably well-paid fashion artist.

Dorian was surprised. So were Pam and Jerry North, who were contentedly having cocktails with Dorian on, as they freely admitted, Pam North's invitation. "Painters," Pam said, "make things impossible." Dorian, who has green eyes and moves with a special grace, said, "Fancy seeing you here," and Bill said, "Fancy," and kissed her.

"I," Pam North said, "can remember when you used to kiss me like that, Jerry. Long, long ago."

"I can remember—" Jerry began and Pam said, "Maybe you'd better not," and flushed slightly, and to herself unexpectedly.

Bill was provided for and the others refreshed. Bill sipped and looked pleased. Then he said he had been trying to get Jerry on the telephone. He was not at the office, not at home.

"Giving an author lunch," Jerry said. "And don't tell anybody what time you tried. And Pam called from here and said the painters were impossible, and she had thrown us both on Dorian's mercy. Why?"

"To ask," Bill said, "whether you've ever come across, or heard of, a man named Carl Cunningham."

Jerry repeated the name. He shook his head. He said, "Should I have?"

Cunningham apparently was, or had been, or had hoped to be, a writer. Jerry was a publisher.

"No," Jerry said. "I can ask around, though. Tomorrow?"

"He lives in Arkansas," Bill said. "Or, did. Years ago. He may have been dead for years—for five years or so, anyway. Up to then he was being helped by Amanda Towne. He—"

Bill told them what he knew about Cunningham.

"Is that all?" Pam asked, when he had finished and, when he nodded his head, said, "It isn't a lot, is it? Unless, when she stopped sending him money, he got mad and—" She shook her head. "It really isn't much," she said. "And Arkansas is so far off." She paused. "Of course," she said, "I do know some people in Hot Springs."

They awaited amplification.

"That's all," Pam said. "I just know some people who live in Hot Springs."

"I do," Jerry said, "hope they like it."

"Oh," Pam said, "very much. Mr. Kingsley is an Arkansan, too." She shook her head. "That can't be right," she said. "Because they don't pronounce it that way. Arkansawer? Sawian? You'd thought of that?"

"That Kingsley comes from Arkansas?" Bill said, circumventing the problem. "Yes. And that, as a writer, he might know other writers in the state. Even much older writers, as Cunningham obviously would be. Know of them, at least. And that Miss Towne also came from Arkansas."

"For what it's worth," Pam said, and Bill, answering, agreed more with her tone than with her words. He said, "Probably nothing."

"You must have more," Dorian said. She sat, her right foot tucked under her left knee, in a deep chair. She sat relaxed as a cat, but with the same readiness.

They had odds and ends, Bill said, and told of them—told of James Fergus and something of what Fergus had told him of the days in Chicago; told of Alice Fleming, and the arrangements she and a man named Bart had made to safeguard Amanda Towne's money; of the continued absence of Judge Roger Parkman and of the interesting trip a man named Tony Gray was about to take, partly because he was unleashed by the death of Amanda Towne. He told of Amanda's liking for a rich and highly flavored tea, and of the color of two of the sofa pillows in her suite.

"Nothing," Dorian said, "to build anything on."

"The red pillows," Pam said. "Meaning she might have been smothered there, with one of them, and carried—or dragged, I suppose—to our room?"

They checked things out, whatever their meaning, or lack of it. Detective Willings had done what was indicated in the checking out.

"It would have been risky," Jerry said. "Taking her along the corridor. Dead."

It would have been. But, murder is a risky business. Among risks it is sometimes necessary to choose the lesser. The premature discovery of a body might well be a greater risk. If, for example, the discovery came too soon after a known visit to a hotel suite. The trouble, however, was that no such visits were known about, independently.

Few things are easier than to pay unnoticed visits to rooms in large hotels, assuming the visitor knows the room he wants. Even preliminary calls on house telephones would be unnoticed, since no records are made of such calls. Nobody, for example, had seen Byron Kingsley, or remembered having seen him. They had checked on that, as a matter of routine. And, of course, of timing.

"He," Pam said, "is much too sweet. Too—sort of loose and gentle. By loose, I don't mean loose, exactly. Un-unknotted? Anyway."

"Also," Jerry said, "he's much too valuable, Bill. He might write another."

Bill was not, he assured them, after their pet author. Kingsley was, for the moment, merely an example of the easy accessibility of hotel rooms. Of course, he was the last known to have seen Amanda Towne alive.

"Except the judge," Pam said. "Or Judd somebody. Is smothering hard? I mean to give, not to receive?"

It was not especially difficult to smother. Circumstances decided. With warning, an able-bodied person—and Amanda Towne had been that—could make it hard for anybody but a much more powerful assailant. Unprepared—perhaps lying back comfortably on a sofa or in a deep chair, or on a bed, there may be little chance for struggle, and almost none for a successful one. Death may come very quickly. And, if the body is not examined for some time, death may appear due to natural causes, and even an autopsy prove inconclusive.

"There isn't even a great deal to guess about, is there?" Dorian said. "Whyn't we have one more round and then somewhere for dinner? Because, all I've got is four lamb chops. Jerry, why don't you, while Bill catches up?"

Jerry did not try to think of a reason. He got gin and vermouth from a refrigerator almost as familiar to him as his own, and a fresh lemon and a chilled mixing pitcher already filled with ice, and poured a few drops of water from the pitcher. He measured, in a two-ounce glass—

"He's the only man I know who can heap liquid," Pam says now and then of Jerry, proudly.

—eight ounces of cold gin and then, with that poured over ice, a very unheaped two ounces of vermouth. He stirred briskly for a moment, sliced strips of lemon, went to the refrigerator for four fresh glasses chilling in the freezing compartment and brought them back carefully, stems between fingers, bowls untouched. (The warmth of hands should not be transferred to frigid glasses.) He poured carefully, evenly, into glasses, twisted lemon peel over the first glass until tiny spatters of oil dimpled the surface, and rubbed the twisted peel around the glass's rim.

"And that," Pam said, "*is* the way to make—"

The telephone rang, with a telephone's uncontrolled excitement. Jerry, too concentrated on perfection, jumped slightly—slightly, but enough. He said, "Oh damn!" and grabbed at a swaying glass, and knocked another over with the movement. He caught both glasses before they fell, but not before they had, largely, emptied themselves.

Dorian Weigand uncoiled, reached the telephone, and said, "Yes?" to it. Then she said, "Just a moment," and held the telephone toward Bill and said, "I thought it was too good to be true."

Bill crossed the room to her, and to the telephone and said, in turn, "Yes? Weigand speaking," and then, "Yes, I did, Mr. Kingsley." He listened a moment. "Oh," he said, "there wasn't any hurry. Good of you to call. Just one question—do you know a man named Cunningham? Carl Cunningham? He's a writer too, I understand. Lives somewhere in Arkansas and—" He stopped and listened. He said, "That's interesting, Mr. Kingsley. I wonder if I could drop around to your hotel and—"

Dorian's slim, long-fingered hands, together, made a beckoning gesture.

"—or," Bill said, "why don't you come over here? The Norths are here and we can give you a drink. If you're not—" Again, it appeared, he was interrupted. He said, after a second, "Right. Take you about ten minutes," and gave the address.

Bill put the telephone back.

"He does know him," he said. "Known him for years. And—saw him in New York yesterday. He's coming over to tell us all about it." He looked at Jerry, who was mopping up. "That," he said gravely, "is *not* the way to make a martini."

Jerry remade. They sipped, and waited.

IX

It took Byron Kingsley a little longer than ten minutes. He wore tweeds; he stooped a little as he came through the doorway, although that was not really necessary. He said hello to the Norths and that it was mighty nice to meet Dorian and Bill Weigand, and that it was mighty nice of them to have him come around. He said, being asked, that a little bourbon and tap water would be fine, if not too much trouble. He looked through windows toward the East River and said they certainly had a wonderful view.

With these matters attended to, he said that he had indeed known Carl Cunningham, far away and rather long ago, and that Mr. Cunningham was a mighty fine man.

"Did you," Bill asked him, "know that Cunningham was an old friend of Miss Towne's?"

Kingsley's wide eyes widened. He shook his tawny head slowly, thoughtfully.

"No," he said. "I didn't know that. Is that why—?"

That, Bill Weigand agreed, was why. Which did not mean that Carl Cunningham was, in any way they now knew of, specifically involved. In the investigation of murder, much is explored that is entirely tangential. This is particularly true when the physical circumstances of the crime are not in themselves revealing, or sufficiently revealing. Then enquiry extended in many directions, in time and space—it was carried into the past and, in a sense, projected into the future—in the sense that murder is sometimes done to prevent an event of the future.

"More simply," Weigand said, "we're trying to find out everything we can about Miss Towne, and about those who've been part of her life. Like Cunningham. You say you saw him in New York yesterday?"

"Well," Kingsley said, slowly, "I'm almost sure I did, captain.

I could—then, anyway—have sworn it was Carl. I yelled at him —said, 'Hey. Carl!' He was getting into a cab. But, either it wasn't Carl or he didn't hear me or—" He paused. "I thought he did hear me. It was as if he started to turn when he heard his name, and then—didn't. But—now I wouldn't want to swear to that, sir. Could be it was just somebody who looked like him."

"Where was this?"

It had been, Kingsley told them, outside the Algonquin. But he was not certain that Cunningham—if it had been Cunningham—had come out of the hotel. At least, he had not been staying at the hotel. Kingsley had asked about that. It had been in mid-afternoon. Kingsley had had lunch at the Algonquin—"with a lady"—after he had signed his statement at the West Twentieth Street station house. He had finished lunch, and got the lady into a cab and it was a few seconds after that that he had seen a familiar figure getting into another cab and called, "Carl! Carl Cunningham." At a guess, it had been around three o'clock.

"Of course," Kingsley said, "I hadn't laid eyes on Carl for years. All the same, I could have sworn—"

But now, he could not swear. It might have merely been a tall man, a tall thin man, who looked like Carl Cunningham. Probably was, because—well, the last he had heard of him, Cunningham was living up in the Bostons.

"The Bostons?"

"Sorry, sir," Kingsley said, like a man at fault. "The Boston Mountains. Part of the Ozarks you can call them. Pretty country, but you get out of towns, off main roads, some of it's pretty wild. Somebody—some naturalist, I think it was—said that the whole Ozark country is one of the best places in the world for snakes. Some of the prettiest snakes you ever saw. Colors you wouldn't think snakes could be. I remember one was the brightest green in the—"

He stopped, evidently feeling that he was failing to hold his audience. Pam, particularly, looked to be an audience on the loose—an audience about to run. Kingsley said he was sorry; that he had got to remembering.

"About Cunningham?" Bill said.

Byron Kingsley, in his slow, soft voice, told them what he had to tell of Cunningham.

He had, he said, encountered him first about ten years before, when Cunningham was giving a course at the state university—a course in fiction writing; one of the extension courses being given in Fayetteville. The classes met in the evenings, twice a week—"a lot of people, all kinds, who thought they wanted to write," Kingsley said. "Kids and right old people, and most of them weren't ever going to. You know how it is, sir." The last was to Jerry North, who certainly knew how it was, and said so.

Kingsley himself, he told them, had then been trying to write for several years—writing, and tearing up what he had written and not, so far as he could see, really getting any place. He hadn't, he said, seen much of others who were trying the same thing. Maybe there weren't many in Arkansas; maybe he just hadn't happened to run into them. He had felt isolated; had felt a need for contact with others who practiced the craft he essayed to enter. The classes at Fayetteville had seemed to promise the fellowship he sought. And, if he was lucky, advice which might help.

He thought, now, looking back, that he had been lucky in meeting Carl Cunningham—in listening to him talk about writing to the class; in talking with him, more specifically, about things he had himself written for the class.

"He didn't," Kingsley said, "try to tell us how to write so much. I mean, he said everybody had to write the way it came to him, and that there weren't really any rules. But there were certain things you tried to do in your own way, and sometimes a person looking at it from outside, understanding what you were trying to do, could tell you where you'd gone off."

They had tried to learn to write by writing. That was Cunningham's way of teaching. "He said, 'You just keep on doing it, whether you feel like it or not.'" Some of the stories—most of them—weren't stories at all, weren't written at all. Most of Kingsley's own were like that, he realized now. But—well, apparently some of his weren't.

"Mr. Cunningham," he said—and now, remembering a former mentor, he spoke of him formally—"seemed to think maybe I had something. Or would have something."

They had, despite their disparity in age—a disparity of some twenty-five years—struck up what amounted to a friendship. Kingsley had taken to going around to Cunningham's room—it wasn't much of a room; the only thing in it that was Cunningham's own, Kingsley thought now, was a pretty "beat-up" typewriter. They talked about writing, and about writers. "I must have bored him, but he didn't show it."

That lasted for two or three years. Kingsley was supporting himself—not too well—by selling brushes, and by whatever else came to hand—whatever else that did not tie him too closely to a fixed way of life, did not interfere too much with his attempt to find his own way.

And then Cunningham had left the university. Kingsley didn't know why—whether he had tired of teaching, on a part-time lecturer's tiny wage, or for other reasons. He had said he was going off somewhere, by himself, and try to get on with his own writing. "Maybe," Kingsley said, "little as I suppose he was getting, he'd saved up some kind of stake." Cunningham had said he was going up in the hills, where living wouldn't cost much, and get on with it.

They had, Kingsley said, kept in touch, more in the first few years after Cunningham left the university than later. "It just sort of petered out, the way those things do." Kingsley had kept on trying to write, without much luck. "What it came to," he said, "I wasn't any good with short stories and pretty soon I decided I wasn't ever going to be. So then I started the novel." He sipped his drink. "The one you saw," he told Jerry North, "was the third shot at it, and part of it was the fourth. And still you and you and Mr. Barry had to pretty near rewrite it, sir."

"Not by miles," Jerry said, although there was some truth in it.

"To get back to Cunningham," Bill said. "How did his own work go? Did he tell you? In letters, I suppose. Before it petered out, as you say?"

Kingsley hesitated. He seemed reluctant. Then he said, "I don't know, sir. I'm afraid—not too good. I kept reading magazines at the library, looking for something by him. And I had a friend in a bookshop and he'd let me go over publishers' announcements. But—I guess it didn't go so good. Maybe he was a better teacher than he was a writer. He—"

Kingsley stopped again.

"Well," he said, "I went up to this place of his once. About three-four years ago. Hell and gone—sorry, ma'am—way up in the hills. You had to park your car about a mile off and climb up a path that wasn't much of a path. And the place he lived—well, you'd have to call it a shack. He—"

Cunningham had looked a good deal older. He had been thin when he gave the course at the university—tall and thin, with thick black hair. He was thinner when Kingsley visited him in the shack. Kingsley had wondered if he was getting enough to eat. He had been thinner and his hair wasn't black any more—what there was of it was gray and— "Well," Kingsley said, "he looked awful."

They had talked, the big, tawny-haired man said, mostly about his own work, and he had admitted that it wasn't coming any too well, and had said that maybe he wasn't cut out for it after all, and had probably better get on with brush-selling.

"He said, 'Don't do that, King.' He called me that, most of the time. A lot of people did. Byron's sort of—well, my dad admired Byron a lot. Used to read him a lot. Anyway, Carl said, 'Just stick to it, King. It's a long way, but you'll make it.' As if he really meant it. Maybe if he hadn't said that, as if he meant it, I would have given the whole thing up—chucked it, as they say. I certainly appreciate what he did for me. What everybody's done."

Kingsley had, of course, asked how Cunningham's own work was going. "Although I guess I was pretty willing to talk about what I was doing most of the time." Cunningham had said he was "getting by" and then turned the conversation back to Kingsley, as if what he himself was doing was of no importance.

"Or, as if he didn't want to talk about it," Kingsley said.

He had stayed a couple of days in the shack with Cunningham, and had driven into town—"if you could call it a town"—and bought a good deal more food than they would need while he was there, and left most of it when he left. Cunningham had smiled faintly at that, but not said anything about it; the acceptance had been tacit, and with it was the tacit admission that the food could be used. So, Kingsley had thought, his friend wasn't "getting by," whatever he said.

There had been several more letters after that—the meeting had, as such meetings sometimes do, revived a relationship which had all but petered out. But then—this was a couple of years ago, when Kingsley had just about decided he could do nothing more with *Look Away, Stranger*, except to start sending it around—a letter he had written had come back with a penciled notation which read, informally—"It wasn't what you'd call a regular post office—'Not here any more.'"

"So," Kingsley said, and had apparently finished, "that's about it. Until—well, unless it was really Carl I saw yesterday. More I think about it, the more I think maybe it wasn't. Because—well, where would he have got the money?"

"You didn't try to find him in Arkansas? After the letter came back?"

"I should have, shouldn't I?" Kingsley said. "I kept thinking I would, but—well, I didn't. It's quite a drive up there—I was living in Little Rock by then and—" He shook his head. "I should have," he said. "I sure should. Maybe I could have—maybe he needed some kind of help. But—I just didn't."

He shook his head, as one may with regret, may self-chidingly.

"He never," Bill said, "talked about his days in Chicago? When he was on the paper there?"

"I knew he had been," Kingsley said. "I suppose he must have mentioned it. But he didn't talk about it, in the way I guess you mean."

"And never," Bill said, "mentioned that he knew Amanda Towne in the old days? Not even after she had become rather famous? Never said, 'I used to know her when'?"

Cunningham never had. Kingsley was sure of that.

Kingsley finished his drink. He waited, looking from one to the other. But, also, he looked at his watch. He said he guessed that was about all he knew about Mr. Cunningham, and—

"We're all going out to dinner pretty soon," Pam North said. "When we finish these." She indicated "these" by wiggling, slightly, her partly filled glass. "If you haven't anything else to do—?"

"Now," Kingsley said, "that's mighty nice of you, Mrs. North. Of all of you. But—fact is, ma'am, I've sort of got a date. With a lady. Supposed to pick her up about—" he looked at his watch again—"about ten minutes from now," he said. "So—"

"Of course," Pam said.

Kingsley stood up. He said he was sorry about the date. He said if he had known but—but there it was. And—

"Run along to your girl, Mr. Kingsley," Dorian said, and he smiled wide and warmly at that and said, "Guess I'd better, ma'am." And, finally, did.

"He's sweet," Pam said. "And doesn't know how to get away once he's somewhere. How old is he, Jerry?"

Somewhere, Jerry thought, in his early or middle thirties. He looked younger; he acted younger. But—

"He does," Dorian said, "bring out the maternal, doesn't he?" She looked at Bill, looked at Jerry. "I can't," Dorian said, "say that ours do, particularly."

"We must," Pam told her, "be thankful for small things. Who wants them boyish? Except in passing, like Mr. Kingsley?"

The men were tolerant; they looked at each other and expressed tolerance. They sipped.

"Why Mr. Cunningham?" Pam asked, of anybody with an answer. "Anyway, I don't quite believe in him."

"I don't—" Jerry said.

"Why pick on him, I mean," Pam said. "You, Bill."

He hadn't, Bill said, picked on him. He hadn't picked on anybody and couldn't argue that he was close to it. But—he did know what Pam meant. And—he did not know why.

"A hunch?" Dorian said.

It was not even that. It was— He paused and sipped reflectively. He didn't, he said, know quite what it was. Unless—you call it a fix. They looked at him with some surprise.

"Not the kind of fix you're thinking of," Bill said.

"For my part," Pam said, "I'm not thinking of any kind. I do wish, Bill, you wouldn't be so—elliptic. What's a fix? Your kind?"

His kind, Bill said, was the "fix" of navigation. From a ship, a bearing taken on, say, one light of known position; simultaneously (or with allowance) a bearing on another. Possibly, even a bearing on a third. Lines drawn on a chart at the bearings indicated. Where the lines crossed on the chart, there was the ship, there were you. There was your "fix."

"I don't think," Dorian said, "that you have made it any clearer, my friend."

It was, Bill admitted readily, not at all clear. You took a bearing on a certain incident in the past—on a certain relationship in the past. Then on another—perhaps one much closer. One point of reference might be a happening; another a thing no more concrete than a facet of character. You drew bearing lines on the chart of your mind. Where they crossed, there—well, there you might be. A line on the mind's chart from Chicago, and a girl's influence on three diverse men; a line from a shack in the hills—the "highlands" of Arkansas; a line from a classroom in Fayetteville, and from a table in a restaurant off Madison Avenue. Where they intersected—

"I can't," Dorian said, "see that they do. Are my wits dull? Or yours fanciful?"

Bill smiled and shook his head, which said he had no answer

ready; which, at the same time, denied the possibility that Dorian's wits were dull.

"Also," Pam said, "there is this judge. There is Mr. Gray's going to Indonesia. There is—"

"Singapore," Jerry said.

"It's the same thing," Pam said, generously. "You've thrown me off. There is Mr. Fergus's maybe getting fired and Miss Towne's brother maybe inheriting a lot of money, if Mrs. Fleming hasn't stolen it and—where do those lines cross?"

They didn't. At least Bill could not, at the moment, see that they crossed. Which was more or less what he was getting at. One could not, obviously, ignore any of these—points of reference. They were not being ignored. Mullins, for example, was hunting for Judge Parkman. Miss Towne's brother was being looked into. Perhaps, from these enquiries—and those into Miss Towne's financial affairs, and even from the papers in her desk—a new pattern might emerge. But, so far he did not see the pattern—did not see bearing lines crossing at a point of space or time or human motivation. Whereas, if one considered Chicago, and Fergus and Cunningham, Barnes and a girl from Arkansas in Chicago; and Arkansas and Byron Kingsley coming out of it—to say nothing of his book—and two people dead in New York—

Well, observations were yet incomplete; bearings needed checking; the mind is more fallible than a pelorus. But he thought the lines showed signs of crossing. At, or near, a man named Cunningham. Who probably—first certainty may be better than second doubt—had been in New York at the proper time.

"I think," Dorian said, "that we had better go and get some dinner."

Bill grinned at her and stood up. As soon as he made a telephone call, he told them and added, as he reached for the telephone, that they were probably quite right. But he called in, all the same and, being in, directed that the proper people in Arkansas—whoever they might be—be got in touch with and asked for co-operation in re one Carl Cunningham, erstwhile college instructor, erstwhile Chicago newspaperman, sometime hermit.

This done, they went to dinner at the Algonquin. Jerry was about to eat an oyster when he remembered something. He put his fork down, with an oyster on it, and said, speaking rather carefully, "Pam. Why don't you believe in Mr. Cunningham?"

She said, naturally, "What?"

"You said," Jerry began and she said, "Oh. That. Everybody drops names."

The three of them looked at Pam North then, in puzzled, but rather pleased, anticipation.

"It's only human," Pam said. "If you've got names to drop, you drop them. I don't care who you are, or how good your intentions. Sooner or later, you drop them."

They continued to wait.

"Miss Towne," Pam said, "was a very good name. I'm not sure she wouldn't be better back there than in New York. Because there aren't so many other things in Arkansas, see?" She stopped and blinked slightly. "It comes out oddly that way," she said. "Anyway—if I'd gone to school with—oh, Elvis Presley—"

"God forbid," Jerry said.

"All right," Pam said. "I agree. I'd drop him, all the same. It would be a—a reflex. But, Mr. Cunningham worked with Miss Towne, and was a friend of hers—and maybe even wanted her to marry him—and she's become famous. And—he doesn't drop her. Not once. So, naturally, I don't believe in him."

"Oh," Jerry said and retrieved his oyster.

Bill Weigand looked at Pam for some seconds. Then he speared an oyster of his own and looked at it. It was, however, a moment or two before he put it in his mouth.

They were at coffee when Raul, shining as a maitre d' should, and regretful as was appropriate, came to report that Captain Weigand was wanted on the telephone. Dorian moaned resignedly in her throat. Bill went to the telephone and returned to report that he would have to drop by the office for an hour or so. "Always," Dorian said. "It never fails."

"You would marry a policeman," Bill told her.

"Nothing else would do," Dorian agreed. Which, come to think back on it, was true. . . .

"This," Sergeant Stein—repatriated from Washington—told Bill Weigand and held this out. "In her desk."

This was a letter, addressed to Amanda Towne, on the letterhead of a television station—"CBC Affiliate"—in Little Rock. It read:

"I'm afraid we haven't been able to dig up much about Kingsley you haven't got. We'd already checked on him, for the local-boy-makes-good angle, and come up with nothing spectacular. He doesn't seem to have known a great many people; those who did know him liked him all right, and didn't see much of him because he was working most of the time—making a living, evidently in any way that came handy, daytimes and writing nights. All his ways of making a living seem to have been drearily legal. He was born in Mississippi, and his family moved to Arkansas when he was about fifteen—hence, I suppose, the Deep South stuff in the book. We're not that deep here, for the most part. I wish we had something juicy to send along for the show. It appears there just isn't anything.

"About Cunningham—and if there's a local angle will you pass it along?—we haven't been able to find out much, either. He did teach a while at the U of A—not actually on the faculty; just a part-time instructor. They don't keep permanent records of those who attend extension classes, so there's nothing to show that Kingsley knew him then. Kingsley was graduated from the university, if that's of value. Cunningham taught there several years later, but Kingsley may have gone to his classes, which were open to anybody who wanted to pay the fees. Apparently, not too many did.

"After he left the university, which would have been about eight years ago, Cunningham moved up into the hills—his mail address was a place called Top Town which isn't a town, actually—a general store and a post office, the hell and gone from anywhere. We sent one of the research boys up there, and he had quite a trip—right out of the twentieth century, I gather, and certainly right off paved roads. (Turned in a special expense account for wear and tear on his car.) The man, who runs the store, and reads the postcards, says, Yes, a man who called himself Cunningham lived around there for a while; lived in the old Nelson place, and he reckons he rented it. Didn't have much to do with the rest of them—city feller, seems like. Came to the store once a week and bought canned goods and coffee, and not very much of either. Figured he was pretty well broke, they did, like you'd figure if he was living in the old Nelson shack.

"I'm trying to paraphrase what the research boy told us—a great guy for dialogue, the boy is. Writes scripts in his spare time, all full of local color.

"Cunningham didn't get much mail, as the storekeeper remembers it. Once a month or so he got a letter from New York, registered. He never happened to notice who the letter came from. None of his business, or anybody else's except Cunningham. The people up there aren't very forthcoming with city people. They probably weren't with Cunningham.

"About three years ago, Cunningham quit coming down to the store. They figured he'd left. Nobody had seen him go, and he didn't have a car, so far as anybody knows. On the other hand, the railroad's only about ten miles away, and anybody could walk it who wanted to. They figured he just walked it.

"I realize we didn't get much, but you weren't very clear what you wanted. I don't know whether we could have got much more if you had been. Nobody seems to remember reading anything Cunningham had written and we haven't found anything in the library. But I suppose you've had that checked in New York."

("Send somebody up to the public library," Bill told Stein, interrupting his reading. "See if a Carl Cunningham shows up in the catalogue index. Oh—the periodical indexes too. Right?")

"Our boy," the letter continued, "got directions and went up to the cabin Cunningham had been living in. It's about a mile, mile and a half, from the nearest road, mostly straight up, on a path which is pretty hard to follow. Our boy says he was all the time meeting snakes coming down the path. The cabin, which apparently isn't much, is on top of a hill, in a clearing that is growing over. There's not much to indicate that anybody has lived in it for years—or, our boy says, ever. He checked with the State police, who'd never heard of anybody named Cunningham and, apparently, had just barely heard of Top Town. And that, I'm afraid is all we've dug up.

"If you hear of an opening for a bright young man in the big town, will you pass it along? And I don't mean to our research genius."

The letter was signed, cordially, "Ned."

Stein had waited for Weigand to finish. Then he said there was a good deal more stuff from Amanda Towne's desk, if Bill wanted to go over it. Bill raised enquiring eyebrows. "Nothing I saw," Stein said. "Then," Bill Weigand said, "why me, sergeant?" This pleased Stein, as it was intended to.

"That help?" Stein said, and indicated the letter.

Bill said he didn't know, and spoke slowly.

"There's nothing in it we didn't know about," he said, and told Stein what they did know, and where it had come from. It accorded with what Kingsley had told, or near enough. It had been "a couple of years ago," Kingsley said, when a letter was returned to him from, it now appeared, Top Town, with the annotation that Cunningham was no longer there. The postmaster said that Cunningham had disappeared three years ago. But the discrepancy was minor; "a couple" is imprecise on the lips of many.

But, all the same, the letter helped. It was an answer to a letter Amanda Towne had written, apparently only a short time before. She had wanted to know about Kingsley, which was understandable; research for interviews, Bill gathered, was thorough. But—she had also wanted to know about Cunningham and had, apparently, been urgent enough in her request to cause the local station to go to considerable trouble. It was to be presumed that the station carried "People Next Door," and that co-operation was in order. Still—Amanda Towne must have been very urgent. Why?

Bill wished he knew the answer. Sergeant Stein, "filled in," wished he could provide it. Meanwhile, did Weigand want the city combed out for Cunningham?

A little reluctantly, since such combing out requires many men, working methodically—and is very likely to be a protracted business, and to end inconclusively—Bill Weigand agreed that he did. Stein made a telephone call to get it started.

"If anything comes in," Bill said, and got up and started toward the door, "I'll be—"

The telephone rang. Stein took it, listened, beckoned Bill Weigand back with a movement of his head.

Sergeant Mullins was calling. He had found Judge Roger Parkman. He had found him very easily—Judge Parkman had come home.

Judge Parkman had nothing to tell them about anything. And he would tell the nothing he had to tell only to the officer in charge. So?

"Right," Bill said, and went back to his desk and said, "What have we got on—" and did not need to finish, because Stein handed him a précis of what they had on Judge Roger Parkman, late of the Court of General Sessions, County of New York.

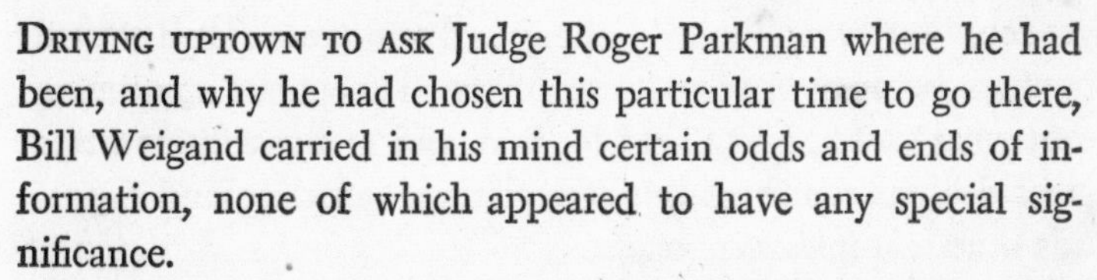

X

DRIVING UPTOWN TO ASK Judge Roger Parkman where he had been, and why he had chosen this particular time to go there, Bill Weigand carried in his mind certain odds and ends of information, none of which appeared to have any special significance.

Judge Parkman, a few years before, had been appointed to fill out the unexpired term of the General Sessions bench of one Antonio Consenti, deceased. Judge Parkman had, as a jurist, expired with the term. (Since he was a Republican, the New York *Times* had regarded his appointment as a commendable example of bi-partisanship, and of getting the best man for the job regardless of political affiliations. The New York *Post*, on the other hand, had darkly regarded the appointment as a "deal" and had wondered, gloomily, what lay behind it. There had, so far as Bill could see, been little in Judge Parkman's conduct on the bench to substantiate either view. His ability had not been flagrantly outstanding; on the other hand, little had occurred to justify the *Post* forebodings.)

Only one controversy, and it minor, had arisen during Parkman's two years and three months as a judge. A certain Marvin Bronsky had been arrested, after patient police work, and had cheerfully admitted that he was indeed the long-sought person who had been building bonfires in churches. He had done it, he explained in magistrate's court, to prove he was right. Bronsky's next stop was, expectedly enough, the psychiatric ward at Bellevue.

He had emerged from Bellevue after some weeks and been brought before Judge Parkman, psychiatrists buzzing about him to explain that his mental condition was such as to leave him unaware that there is anything wrong in building bonfires in churches—that, specifically, he was incompetent to enter a plea to the indictment. Judge Parkman had then, rather unexpectedly, proved himself to be made of sterner stuff. He had expressed himself firmly against coddling and directed that a plea be entered. He happened to be looking at Bronsky when he made this demand and Bronsky, before his court-appointed lawyer could intervene, smiled happily and said that he had started bonfires because bonfires were pretty. The judge, spluttering somewhat, ordered him held for trial, and said that there was a great deal too much of this sort of thing going on and that it was time examples were made.

The effect on Bronsky himself of this difference of opinion, with Parkman on one side and science on the other, was nonexistent. Bronsky had started bonfires also in Brooklyn churches, and a Kings County judge took a look at him and had him sent to Matteawan. But Parkman had had his moment.

A good many letters were written to newspapers about the incident, and all those in the *Herald Tribune* and most of those in the *Times* agreed with Judge Parkman that it was indeed high time, that even-handed justice (as personified in Judge Parkman) should be exercised, and that if "do-gooders" had their way, as they had had ever since Franklin Delano Roosevelt was mistakenly allowed to occupy the White House, the moral fiber of the country would be left in tatters. "Must We Coddle Criminals?" the *Journal American* asked, in a vigorous editorial, and concluded that we mustn't.

Whether this example of judicial highmindedness was a major factor in Judge Parkman's subsequent, if unfortunately brief, rise to favor in party ranks could only be guessed about. Judge Parkman had other suitable attributes. He was a rich man, for one thing, and he had made frequent and gratifying contributions to party funds; he was a corporation lawyer of reasonable standing before his elevation to the bench, and again after his descent from it. He was a vestryman of note; his advocacy of what were termed "right to work" laws was as firm as his rejection of minimum wage laws was vigorous. He had taken an unwavering stand against rent control legislation and, while he recognized the place of labor unionism in the social scheme, he warned that many unions had long since stepped out of it.

In short, Judge Parkman had appeared a natural for a nice nomination—lieutenant governor, perhaps—until he had responded with too little caution to the gentle promptings of Amanda Towne. That, it was generally felt in political circles, had done him in. The firmest rejection of coddling, of the welfare state, was thereafter not enough. To win as a Republican in New York State it is necessary to pick up at least some votes in New York City. And New York City is polyglot, and varicolored. Unless the whole matter blew over, which it was not going to if the Democrats could help it, Judge Parkman had had it.

Judge Parkman might well, Bill Weigand thought, ringing the doorbell of a sedate and private house on one of the best blocks in the East Sixties, have taken a dislike to Amanda Towne. Even a rather violent dislike. But still—

"Is Judge Parkman in?" Bill asked a butler, who looked at him with austerity.

"I will have to—" the butler began, and Bill said, "Captain Weigand. Of the police." To that, the butler said, "Oh," in a disparaging tone, but opened the door a little wider. Bill went into a foyer and found Sergeant Mullins sitting there, in what amounted to outer darkness, facing sliding doors which were closed against him. Mullins sat on a small wooden chair with a knobby back—a chair not really planned for sitting on. He stood up, thankfully, when Bill came in and they waited while the butler knocked at the sliding doors and then, encouraged by a "Yes?" from within, opened only one of them—there were gradations in these matters, Bill thought with amusement—and said, "A man from the police, sir."

There was a snort from beyond the door.

"Judge Parkman will see you," the butler said, with the air of one who cannot imagine why. Bill Weigand led the way through the door and Mullins went after him. The butler looked at Mullins sharply; Mullins returned the look. The butler drew back a little, enlarging the aperture.

Judge Parkman was a big man—a big man with a ruddy face and white hair and an expression of indignation which seemed, Bill thought, to have found permanent tenancy.

"So you're the one," Judge Parkman said, without rising from a deep leather chair. "What is the explanation?"

"Explanation?" Bill repeated, and was bland. "Of what, judge?"

He was told he knew very well what. He was told that he had exceeded his authority.

"Prying into my private affairs," Judge Parkman said. "Snooping around among my associates. Permitting these men of yours" —he glared at Mullins, with that—"to make slanderous implications." He glared at Bill. "You may as well know," he said, "that I have consulted counsel."

"Right," Bill said. "Very understandable. And—he advised that you return home, didn't he, judge? To answer whatever proper questions we might want to ask, since you have nothing to hide?"

"It is," Judge Parkman said, "none of your concern what passed between myself and my legal adviser. As a police officer, you should know that."

"Right," Bill said again. "Nevertheless, you have returned home. Do you mind telling me why you left so—precipitately?"

"Yes," Judge Parkman said. "I do mind. And—what do you mean precipitately? I decided to take a few days' rest. To get away from busybodies. People who are trying to make political capital out of—" He stopped abruptly, apparently feeling that he was once again saying more than he would be wise to say. "And I hear that your people are nosing around in my private affairs," he said. "Among my associates. Well?"

He glared up at Bill Weigand, who looked down at him with no special expression.

"Suppose," Bill said, "I put it to you this way, judge. That you know quite well we are making an investigation of the murder of a woman named Amanda Towne. Of her husband, a man named Russell Barnes. A few hours after Barnes is killed, you—"

Judge Parkman's face turned very red indeed—so red that Bill was reminded of Deputy Chief Inspector Artemus O'Malley. He thought that, on the whole, he much preferred O'Malley.

"You have the effrontery to stand there—" Judge Parkman said, and this time Bill Weigand interrupted.

"Yes," he said. "You were—probably—encouraged to make certain statements during an interview with Miss Towne. As a result of these statements—or, say, of the interpretation put on them—there was a good deal of talk. Adverse talk. Adverse to your political—ambitions."

"I," Judge Parkman said, and now spoke a little as if he were addressing a meeting, "have no political ambitions. If called upon by my party to—"

"Right," Bill said. "I don't say you have. Or had. It would, I'd think, be natural, in any case and under the circumstances, if you felt some resentment toward Miss Towne. Perhaps a great deal of resentment. Perhaps you even felt that she was—put up to it?"

"I wouldn't put it past people like that," Judge Parkman said. "Everybody knows that people like that are a bunch of Communists at bottom. Communistic eggheads. Read *Red Channels*. Got it down in black and—" He stopped. He stared at Weigand. "How about you?" he demanded. "Wouldn't be the first policeman."

Bill Weigand kept his temper. This was something of a strain.

"I know nothing about Miss Towne's—political background," he said, evenly. "Not that it has anything to do with the matter. Obviously, you disliked her. She was killed. At almost the same time you leave your house. Nobody knows where you've gone. Or admits knowing. Your wife doesn't. Naturally, we try to get in touch with you. You must have realized we'd want to talk to you. Along with a good many other people."

"When I left here," Judge Parkman said, "to get away from all this tempest in a teacup, I didn't know that the Towne woman was dead. Or that even a bungling policeman would think that I—*I* would have any information to give. Mrs. Parkman, of course, knew where I had gone. And why."

"Then," Bill said, "she wasn't frank with the police, was she? You've been a judge and—"

"I didn't know you people would be nosing around," Parkman said. "How would I? I don't say I'd have suggested—anyway, I'm here now."

Because his lawyer told him to be, Bill thought. Or—because he had arranged a story?

"Do you mind saying where you were?"

"Yes. I do mind."

"Right," Bill said. "Leave that for the moment. Where were you Wednesday evening? Between, say, seven and around nine or so?"

Judge Parkman shook his head. He was quieter now. His eyes, which had been suffused, were sharper, now, and narrower. "No," he said. "No concern of yours."

"Right," Bill said. "Did you, at a little after seven, telephone Miss Towne at her apartment at the Breckenridge? Agree either to join her there, or to meet her some place else?"

"That's preposterous."

"Did you?"

"Certainly not. Why would I want to see her? The fat was in—certainly not." His eyes were very narrow now. "Does somebody say I did?"

"We," Bill told him, "have certain information."

"Your information is inaccurate. Or—somebody is stringing you along."

Bill merely looked at him.

"Yes," Parkman said, and spoke with confidence. "Before you go farther out on a limb. I can prove where I was. If it becomes necessary."

"You don't think it's necessary now?"

"I do not, captain."

"I suppose," Bill said, "the same answer applies to the next afternoon? From, say, about four o'clock on? From then until you packed a suitcase and left here, and told your wife—and the butler, I suppose—not to say where you could be found?"

"Yes. For the time being, at any rate."

"Did you know Barnes? Russell Barnes. A copyreader on the *Globe-Dispatch?*"

"No."

"Didn't run into him at the Breckenridge Wednesday evening? At his wife's apartment, for example?"

"No. You're wasting time, aren't you? Yours and mine?"

"Apparently," Bill said. "You're a lawyer. You've been a judge. As a police officer, I ask you to co-operate."

"Very proper phrasing," Judge Parkman said. "No. I have no information which would assist in your investigation. You get that down, sergeant?"

Mullins looked at him with disfavor. Mullins said, "Yes."

"Get this down," Judge Parkman said. "I categorically deny any knowledge of the circumstances surrounding the deaths of Mrs. Amanda Barnes, known also as Amanda Towne, and Russell Barnes, reputedly her husband. Have you got that down?"

"Yes," Mullins said, although he had not touched pencil to paper.

"Then," Judge Parkman said, and stood up—a large and heavy man, with a face again suffused—"get the hell out of here. Both of you."

"Right," Bill said.

"And stay the hell out of my affairs."

"No," Bill said. "You know better than that, judge."

"So now, loot?" Mullins said, in the car outside. "It 'ud be a pleasure."

Weigand did not need to ask what would give Sergeant Mullins pleasure. He agreed entirely.

"We keep after it?" Mullins said, and Bill said, "Right. For the time being."

"So you don't," Mullins said. "I guess I don't either. All the same, it 'ud be a pleasure."

He turned on the radio and the car was filled with the grating of police talk. None of it appeared to concern them.

Bill drove Mullins to the nearest subway, told him to knock it off for the night, and drove himself home. He had rather expected to find the Norths, fugitive from painters, still there, but he did not.

"Jerry decided he had to go home and read something," Dorian explained. "Was it important, Bill?"

"Miss Towne had been trying to get information about Cunningham," Bill told her. "Judge Parkman didn't do it, he says."

She looked up at him.

"I'm afraid he's right," Bill said. "Although as Mullins says, it would be a pleasure."

"Dear Mullins," Dorian said. "Such a right-thinking man," and reached her hands up. Bill pulled her from the chair, and to the place she belonged. Presently, when the opportunity arose, she suggested they might merely take the telephone off the hook.

"If," Bill said, "I weren't a policeman."

It couldn't be helped, Dorian said—Dorian, who, a fairly long time ago now, had fought against his being a policeman, and against herself and, losing, won. It was surprising, they both thought, and neither needed to say, how little difference years really made in things which mattered most.

***

Pamela North dreamed she was being smothered by, of all people, Deputy Chief Inspector Artemus O'Malley. He was pressing a pillow over her face and, however much she struggled—and she struggled with every nerve and muscle—she could not get free of the pillow, or back to the air again. But then there was a loud sound—somebody had shot Inspector O'Malley, obviously and just in time—and a dazzling light.

"You'll catch your death," Jerry said, looking at his wife, who—fighting against the pillow of death—had writhed out of covers, and more.

"O'Malley tried to kill me," she told him. "Only it was the

paint, I suppose. But you shot him just in time. *Jerry!* Why on earth aren't you asleep? Instead of shooting people and turning on lights?"

She pulled bedclothes up.

"Oh," Jerry said, returning to the matter at hand. "I want you to read something."

"*Read* something?" Pam said. "At this—" she looked at the watch on her wrist—"hour," she said. "Two o'clock in the morning. I know you're a publisher and everything but— What?"

Jerry held a fairly heavy book, and held fingers between pages. He opened the book and said, "Start at the top of this page." He sat down on his own bed, and lighted a cigarette and watched her read.

"My goodness," Pam said, at the bottom of the page, and looked up at Jerry.

"Go ahead," he told her, morosely, and she went ahead. "Oo-h!" Pam said at the middle of the next page, and at the bottom of the third she said, "Ouch." She read on; Jerry had stubbed out his cigarette by the time she lowered the book and looked at him.

"Something, isn't it?" Jerry said. "I remembered it vaguely, and it took quite a while to find it."

"He can do something about it, can't he?" Pam said.

"And," Jerry North said, "how."

"Kingsley agrees—what's the phrase?—'to hold you harmless against any claim' or whatever it is. Isn't that in the contract?"

It was in the contract. It was always in the contract.

"And all the same," Jerry said, "he can sue the shirts off our backs."

He reached over and picked the book up from Pam's bed and looked at it with resentment—a resentment as deep as love had once been deep.

He put *Look Away, Stranger*, by Byron Kingsley, on the table between their beds, and handled it as if it burned his fingers.

***

It took a long time to arouse Tony Gray on Saturday morning. Bill Weigand put his finger on the bell push and kept it there, and heard the bell shrilling in the apartment, but heard nothing else. He tried knocking, and was unanswered. He tried the bell again—Gray slept soundly, or was not at home. Or might, of course, be dead, which would really tie things—and especially Deputy Chief Inspector Artemus O'Malley—into knots.

Tony Gray opened the door, wearing the bottom half of pajamas and an expression of outrage. He was by no means dead. He was bristlingly alive; his red hair bristled. "What the hell?" he demanded, in the anguished tone of a man much put upon. But then he said, "Oh—*you*."

"Yes," Bill said. "Sorry, Mr. Gray."

"Just an hour ago," Gray said, "I finally got to sleep. What do you want at this—this obscene hour?"

The hour was a little short of nine o'clock. Bill, however, felt sympathy. He repeated that he was sorry. He wanted what he always wanted, information. What did Mr. Gray know about a man named Cunningham?

Gray repeated the name. He said he didn't know a thing. He amplified. But then he said that Weigand might as well come in. Weigand went in. "Who's Cunningham?" Gray asked. "Never heard of him."

Cunningham was an old friend of Amanda Towne. He lived in Arkansas, or had. He might now be in New York. Miss Towne had been trying to get in touch with him—trying through contacts in Little Rock, and, it appeared, getting nowhere. Presumably—or, at any rate, possibly—she had hoped to get further background information for her interview with Byron Kingsley. Kingsley had known Cunningham.

"All news to me," Gray said. "And—that's sort of funny. I suppose that's why you're around at this nauseating hour?"

It was. Gray had been gathering information on Kingsley, preliminary to the interview which had never been held. Wouldn't he, in the normal course, have been the one to probe further into Kingsley's background, if further probing was indicated?

"You're damn right," Gray said. "It's sort of funny. I'll give you that. Standard order of procedure, she gave me a name, and said, 'Research him.' If it was a him. And, left it to me."

She had issued the instructions in this case but, apparently, she had not actually left it to him. He had done the usual things —got biographical material from the publicity department of North Books, Inc., read "that damn long book" for Mandy and marked passages she might want to quote, to reveal that intimate knowledge of a work of literature so desirable in one who interviews its author; had himself talked to Kingsley at some length, seeking personality "gimmicks," making notes thereon and submitting the results to Amanda Towne.

"Asked her what more she wanted," he said. "Did she think I'd missed anything? She said she'd go through it and let me know and, next day or so, said she had and that she thought we had plenty. Nothing about any special angle in the past, or in Arkansas. Nothing about anybody named Cunningham."

"That was unusual?"

"If she was on to something, it was. If she thought there was something juicy to be found out about a subject in—hell, in Timbuktu—she'd like as not send me there. But not this time." He pawed his red hair. "I don't get it," he said. "Not like Mandy. Did she get anything hot?"

It did not appear that she had. She had not, certainly, got Cunningham, who apparently had disappeared. Gray couldn't, from his knowledge of Amanda Towne, guess what she had been after?

He could not. It was a new wrinkle to him. He supposed she had had something under her hat; something she wanted to keep there. All he could say was, it wasn't like her. Who had she got to check this Cunningham out, or try to?

Weigand did not know. All he knew was that the letter, obviously an answer to a letter of hers, had been signed "Ned." Gray shook his head at that; said he didn't know anybody named "Ned" either. But, if she wrote to the Little Rock station for information, there had, obviously, been nothing particularly secret about what she wanted.

"Except," Gray said, "from me. I guess from all of us actually working on the show." He shook his head again; again said that it was a funny thing. "Must have had something she thought was hot," he said. "Wanted to spring it on us."

Weigand agreed, and again regretted having wakened Tony Gray (who said, "Oh, the hell with that") and went. It appeared, certainly, that Amanda Towne had wanted to spring something on somebody.

The "In" basket was heavy with paperwork, much of which had nothing to do with the Towne-Barnes case. That, Weigand put aside. There was alibi data, and Bill glanced at that. Everybody had been some place other than the Towne suite on Wednesday evening and Russell Barnes's apartment on Thursday afternoon. Which was to be expected; which was in one case not true. (If, of course, any of the people so far questioned was involved, in itself by no means certain.) If one of the alibis was concocted, they eventually would turn to the matter of cracking it. There was no special point in that until they knew which one to put in the jaws of the cracker.

Detective Freddy Willings had, apparently, been right in his hunch. One of the red sofa pillows from Amanda Towne's suite had disclosed traces of lipstick—type and brand identified, and identified as that used by Amanda Towne. It also disclosed traces of face powder.

And this, of course, did not really prove anything. A woman may get powder, and lipstick too, on pillows in her apartment. Still—

There was the final, complete, report of the autopsy on the body of Amanda Towne. Asphyxia by smothering was proved and— Bill studied a paragraph. Almost microscopic fragments of cotton fiber had been found in the lungs, dragged there—it could be assumed—in the final desperate reaching of the lungs for air. Magnified, tested, they appeared to be from a red dyed fabric. The material appeared, in short, to have been scuffed from, inhaled from, the fabric which covered the pillows. (See supplementary correlated report.) Material had been forwarded to the fiber laboratory of the FBI for verification.

Detective Willings's hunch now looked very good indeed. Weigand drummed briefly with his fingers on his desk top. It appeared that somebody had taken a long chance in a hotel corridor. Presumably because the alternative chance was longer still. Or, had seemed so, with the maid approaching from room to room. And, ironically, had not been.

He reached again to the "In" basket.

A Carl Cunningham, giving his address as Little Rock, Arkansas, had checked in at a large, medium-price, hotel in the theatrical district at ten forty-three the night of Wednesday, November 13. He had checked out at seven-thirty on the morning of Saturday, November 16—half an hour before the precinct man had got there. He had arrived without reservation. No description of any value was available from anyone in the hotel. (The bellman who had taken him to his room thought he had had one suitcase, and thought he was tall, and knew that he had taken dozens of men to rooms that Wednesday night.) Cunningham had printed his name on the registration blank. His room had rented for seven dollars, single. He had signed for no meals and made no telephone calls.

So—assuming it was the right Carl Cunningham, which was an assumption worth precisely nothing. The room he had occupied was being cleaned when the precinct man arrived. That had been stopped, probably too late.

The telephone rang. Bill picked it up and said he was speaking and heard a familiar voice.

"Bill," Jerry North said, "have you got anything on this man Cunningham? Know where he is?"

"No," Bill said, and listened to Jerry North swear with bitterness. When Jerry paused, Bill Weigand said, "Why, Jerry?"

"Because," Jerry North said, "thanks to a blithering jackass named Kingsley, Mr. Cunningham has got us where it hurts. If he wants to. And you can be damn sure he does want to. Because—look, can you come up to the office? Or can I come down there?"

"I'm—" Bill said.

"And also," Jerry said, "the idol of the literary world, the darling of Book-of-the-Month, seems to have taken it on the lam. As you would say."

"No," Bill said. "I almost never do. You're sure?"

"You're damn right," Jerry said. "Checked out. His lecture-agent says he's gone south—Savannah, he thinks, or maybe Jacksonville or maybe God-knows-where, for a long weekend with some new friends. That's what his agent says. But it looks to me—"

"I'll come up to your office," Bill Weigand said. "Take a Miltown. Right?"

"Right," Jerry said. "I think North Books is in a hell of a spot."

North Books, Inc., did not seem in a spot of any kind when Bill walked into its office suite. It seemed calm enough. There was, indeed, no one in it—except in the office of Gerald North, president and editor. There there was little calm. Jerry had not followed advice. He was untranquilized.

He said, "That rat," and then, pointing at a book open on his desk, swinging it to face Bill Weigand, "Read that. Just read it." Jerry thereupon ran his fingers through his hair. Bill read as directed. When he had read a page he whistled softly. When he had read four pages, he looked up at Jerry, and saw that Jerry's face was stricken. Bill went back and reread.

Since *Look Away, Stranger* was a serious novel, and with a Southern locale to boot, it was not entirely clear what, precisely, was going on in the scene which ran from page ninety-three through page ninety-seven. Murkiness predominated; one moved with the author through a fog of allusion, and partly (Weigand assumed) in the present and partly (if he was any judge) in the past. But enough was clear—too much was clear.

The character who, to a degree, emerged from the encircling gloom was one "Carl Connington"—a tall thin man, with long black hair; a former Chicago newspaperman (Bill Weigand was almost sure) and a one-time instructor at a State university. (Bill was quite sure of that; the fact was almost explicit in the narrative.) "Connington" was also a writer; he lived in a shack which seemed to be many miles from anywhere—either in mountains, or in a swamp. And—he was hiding there. Whether he hid from the law, or from private retribution, was not a decision readily made—Byron Kingsley was, most evidently, not a man to blurt things out. But it was clear that, in one fashion or another, a nefarious past was about to catch up with "Carl Connington." It was also clear that "Connington" had coming whatever was coming.

It seemed most likely, after second reading, that "Connington" was a murderer. A murderer at best, and what at worst hardly bore thinking about. Bill Weigand, as he reread the last page, considered—as it were, tried on "Connington" for size—the various evil deeds of which mankind is capable; reflected (between the lines) on the less savory activities of ancient Grecian kings and those, equally numerous if less poetically described, of modern New Yorkers. There was also, of course, the Marquis de Sade.

"What had he done, actually?" Bill asked, when he had finished.

"What?" Jerry said, and then, "Oh—it never does come clear. Not to me, anyway. Murder, at least. Toward the end a couple of men—maybe cops, maybe gangsters, maybe just symbolic monsters—come and take him away. At a guess, he killed somebody in Chicago. Kingsley is one of those authors who says what he's written will have to speak for itself. But—that isn't the point. Not to me."

"No," Bill Weigand said, "I can see it wouldn't be."

"Almost the same name," Jerry said. "The same description, apparently. The same past—Chicago, teaching. The same—" A kind of wail had entered his voice. He heard it; he broke off. He steadied himself.

"If," he said, "there is actually a man named Cunningham and he has done the things this Fergus of yours says he has, and looks the way Kingsley says he does, he can sue the shirt off my back. Invasion of privacy, aggravated libel."

"Your shirt," Bill said. "And Kingsley's? Not just his? Isn't there something in the contract—"

He did not finish, because Jerry was gloomily shaking his head. Oh, there was something in the contract. But, in practice, it represented hardly more than a publisher's pious hope. Of course, Kingsley would be sued; he and North Books, Inc., would be sued jointly. For, Jerry unhappily thought, millions. If there really was a Cunningham—if people were not making him up—

"A man named Cunningham has been in town," Bill said. "He checked into a hotel Wednesday and checked out this morning. We're trying to find him."

Jerry had not doubted there would be a Carl Cunningham, or that he would answer the description of the "Carl Connington" of Kingsley's book—or that he was now somewhere taking matters up with a lawyer, which was no doubt what he had come to New York to do. Unless—

"Of course," Jerry said, "if he killed Amanda Towne. To say nothing of her husband. That would help a lot."

"Right," Bill said. "I can see that. Or—if he really did kill somebody in Chicago years ago."

"There is," Jerry said, "no use looking on the bright side of things." He put his head in his hands. "*Authors!*" he said. "The most irresponsible— The most impossible— Working off old grudges without the least idea that—"

He continued in this strain for some time. Bill Weigand listened with sympathy, having little else to offer.

XI

JERRY NORTH HAD GONE to the office on Saturday morning to be alone with his thoughts, and because Pam had, in any case, an appointment to have her hair done. She offered to cancel the appointment; she suggested that it would save money, which apparently was going to be of the essence, if she did her own hair. They had not, Jerry told her, come yet to so desperate a pass. They would, he promised her, fight to the last ditch. She had gone doubtfully, but she had gone.

When Bill Weigand left, and could do no more than hope, for Jerry's sake, that Cunningham, the illusive, was also Cunningham, the murderer, Jerry remained for some time alone with his thoughts. He told himself sad stories of the bankruptcy of publishers; considered how he would work out as a janitor—or perhaps a night watchman—and what he would do to Byron Kingsley when he got his hands on him. (This was not as cheering as it might have been; he remembered that Kingsley was, after all, a very large man.) He thought that, when it comes to matters of libel, publishers are at the mercy of authors, who may pay old grudges off under thin disguise. *Thin!* Kingsley had, evidently, made no effort whatever to disguise the identity of Carl Cunningham, the "real person" and "Carl Connington," the—whatever he was. Torturer of small children, probably—

One could think that Kingsley—the this-and-that, the so-and-so—had deliberately with malice aforethought, invited this. Except that nobody—not even a novelist—goes out of his way to have the shirt sued off his back. Not even to spite a publisher, who will similarly lose his. Unless he so hates the publisher that—

Jerry entertained only briefly the thought that Byron Kingsley had aimed this hidden knife at his particular back. *Look Away, Stranger* had been to other publishers before it came to him;

Kingsley could not have known at whom he struck. It could hardly be that he so resolutely hated publishers as a race. Of course, to hear some authors talk—

Jerry rejected the notion. Even an author has regard for his own nose. And yet—and yet there was something so overt about the Cunningham-"Connington" device—something so flagrant—

Jerry North stopped against the blank wall of a startling idea. It was impossible. It was unheard of. It was—it was not impossible, even if unheard of. The more he thought—

The telephone on his desk, plugged through from the switchboard, shrilled at him. He grabbed for it. Perhaps Bill had found Cunningham; perhaps Cunningham had admitted—

"Jerry," Pam said. "Are you all right?"

"Oh," Jerry said. "I guess so. Are you done already?"

"Jerry," Pam said. "I looked at the charge slip. I never thought of doing that before and—"

"Never mind," Jerry said. "We'll sink with flags flying. And hair curled. Lunch?"

"Of course," Pam said. "I'll open a can of something nutritious. Beans? Only—the painters are still here. In the kitchen, now."

He had not meant that. He had meant lunch out. As if nothing had happened, as if the heavens still arched.

"An Automat," Pam said. "The food is really very good and—"

"I know," Jerry said. "The food is admirable. The Algonquin. In about—about how long?"

"We shouldn't," Pam said. "Fifteen minutes."

Jerry needed the martini, brought in a glass damp with cold, by Raul himself. It did him good. The second did him better.

"How much do they charge for martinis here?" Pam asked, looking with reproach. That anything so delicious should cost what it probably did!

"I don't know," Jerry said. "Forget it a minute. They could have been in cahoots."

Pam put her glass down carefully. She looked at Jerry with concern.

"Cahoots?" Pam said and then, quite unintentionally, "Ca-who?"

"Cunningham and Kingsley," Jerry said, precisely as if "ca-who" was the word he had been expecting. "Listen, Pam. Suppose—"

Suppose a novelist and another person, both unscrupulous, enter into conspiracy to defraud. The other person offers his person, his good name. The novelist provides the craft.

Carefully, with intent not really to disguise, the novelist draws a character from life—from the life of his co-conspirator. He disguises the name only slightly—as "Carl Connington" for Carl Cunningham. He describes real physical characteristics as precisely as his skill permits. He is equally meticulous in reproducing actual incidents in the life of his confederate. But, to the actual, once the parallel is established beyond question, the novelist adds aspersion of a libelous nature. His fictional character may be an undiscovered murderer; perhaps an escaped convict; certainly a person reprehensible in character and suspect in action. (These things must not, of course, really correspond—a murderer in real life is not libeled if made a murderer in fiction.)

Then—get the novel published. Then—the confederate sues. He sues, of course, both novelist and publisher. Any sums recovered from the novelist are only a matter of arithmetic. Any money recovered from the publisher is shared, at a ratio agreed upon. Everybody is happy—except, to be sure, the mulcted publisher.

"H-mmm," Pam said. "Has it ever been done?"

Jerry did not know that it ever had been done. Or, conversely, that it had not. He could not see any reason why such a fraud could not be carried out.

"Wait," Pam said. "I don't think Mr. Kingsley would—"

"If he isn't a crook," Jerry said, "he is an irresponsible half-wit. He—"

"Wait," Pam said. "Aside from that. I don't think he's that kind of man, but aside from that. He's already made a lot of money out of the book. He's going to make a lot more. Particularly when the movie payments come through. If Cunningham sues—even if he threatens to sue—the movie company will run like a scared rabbit. And, if he won, couldn't he make you stop publishing the book? Wouldn't he *have* to?"

"Yes," Jerry said. "The movie sale is off. The book is called in. We go bankrupt. And Kingsley loses more than he gains. But—*he wouldn't know that in advance.* Nobody could tell that *Look Away, Stranger* was going to turn out the way it did. It might have sold—oh, three or four thousand. All they needed, really, was to get it published." He finished his second drink. "As a matter of fact," he said, "it's the only sure way I know to make money out of writing a book."

Pam said, "H-mmm," and sipped. Then, suddenly, her eyes widened. She said, "Jerry!" and went on without pause.

"Don't you see," Pam North said, "if it was that way—he *won't* sue. Because it's a golden goose. I mean—eggs. Nobody breaks golden eggs. They would have thought of that if they were as scheming as you think. Wait—that's why they haven't sued already. Because—"

"My God," Jerry said. He looked at Pam with admiration, and, inwardly at himself with chagrin. Of course, she was right. For a moment the world brightened. But it then occurred to Jerry North that this might very well be a false dawn, resulting from the acceptance of theory as fact. It might be that the scheme to defraud existed only in Jerry's mind. In which case—

Jerry looked fixedly away. It happened that his fixed gaze seemed, to a bartender across the room, to be fastened on him. The bartender smiled cheerfully, nodded, and began to mix. The movement unfixed Jerry's gaze. Well, it didn't matter. He hadn't felt the first two. He guessed. Pam, far away, was saying something. He said he was sorry, and what?

"—with the murder," Pam said. "Do you think we really ought to, when they're so expensive?"

"It doesn't matter," Jerry said. "Probably we're just pretending there was this scheme. Probably he'll sue any minute now.

For hundreds of thousands, including punitive damages. What murder?"

She looked at him; her eyes asked if he was sure he needed another martini.

"Oh," Jerry said, "*that* murder," and spoke as if there were many to choose from. "What about it?"

"Only," Pam said, "I don't see how this scheme you've ferreted out—and it was clever of you, dear—ties in with killing poor Miss Towne."

"There's no use kidding ourselves," Jerry said. "Probably there wasn't any scheme. Why does it have to tie in with murder, anyway? Except of North Books, Inc.?"

"Neater," Pam said. "When things come up at the same time, it's much neater if they are tied together. Of course, the world isn't very neat, for the most part. Still—"

The drinks came. They looked at them despondently. Jerry reached for his and Pam said, "Wait." He waited.

"It could be," Pam said, "that Miss Towne found out about this scheme somehow. Because of something in the past. Or merely from recognizing that "Carl Connington" was really Carl Cunningham. It could be that she was going to bring it up in the interview with Kingsley. And that she was killed so she wouldn't."

It was Jerry's turn to say "h-mmm." He said it. Then he said that the trouble with that was obvious. If there had been a scheme concocted by Kingsley and Cunningham, circumstances had made it unprofitable. As Pam herself had just pointed out. With this said, he sipped, unhappily.

"I suppose so," Pam said, but then, once again, said, "Wait, Jerry." He put his drink down and waited.

"Something we haven't thought of," Pam said. "Suppose she had found out. Was going to—well, trick Mr. Kingsley into admitting it on the air. Don't you see? Then Mr. Cunningham would *have* to sue. Or admit that he was "Connington," and had done whatever "Connington" was supposed to have done. What was it, by the way? I never did get it clear."

"Murder," Jerry said. "At least, I'm pretty sure."

"Then," Pam said, "he couldn't *not* sue. But if he did, and won—he would win?"

Jerry didn't see how he could fail to win, if the Cunningham they had been told about was an actual person, and "Connington" his image in fiction's mirror.

"And if he won," Pam said, "they would lose heaven knows how much. A lot more than they could actually get out of you, because—"

"I know," Jerry said. "Because it's a lot more than we've got. And—killed Miss Towne because she could have put them in a position where Cunningham *had* to sue? And Barnes because he made the same identification? Or, she'd told him about it and what she planned to do. You know, Pam—"

"See how much neater it is?" Pam said, pleased.

Which brought Jerry down again—down from the pleasures of abstract logic to the jagged rock of fact. All they really knew was that a man named Carl Cunningham had almost certainly been libeled, and flagrantly, in a novel published by North Books, Inc., and would have the recourse the law permits. In other words, bankruptcy.

"It's very neat, Pam," Jerry said. "Maybe we can get a settlement out of court. One that will let us keep our cat."

She patted his hand. She said she'd like to see anybody try to get their cat. She said that, anyway, it would be something to take up with Bill that evening.

Jerry raised eyebrows.

"Don't you remember?" Pam said. "It's their Saturday."

***

It was late afternoon before they found out where Carl Cunningham had gone after he checked out of his hotel in the early morning.

By that time, they had found out, by slow and methodical work, that Judge Roger Parkman had had dinner on Wednesday evening with a blonde. At least, they had found a blonde who said he had, and seemed to have no special reason to lie about it (although about that nobody could be sure) and fixed times which, if accurate, proved Judge Parkman no murderer of, at any rate, Amanda Towne. His whereabouts at the time of the murder of Russell Barnes was still not established.

They had found out that the late Russell Barnes had made a telephone call on Thursday from a lunchroom where he was known—because he went there five days a week, and always early—and the estimated time of this call coincided with the call Pam North had answered while under a sofa.

A Mr. Lovelace had reached his home in Galveston that morning, having tarried on business, and had turned in his key to the suite subsequently occupied by the Norths at the Hotel Breckenridge when he checked out. And had certainly not had it copied while in his possession and what the hell was it all about? By that time, it was about nothing of interest.

Alice Fleming had cheerfully made Amanda Towne's financial records available to the police, and Orson Bart, Amanda's agent, had made his records, in so far as they concerned Amanda, available too, although not as cheerfully. But he was not, generally, in a cheerful mood, having just lost ten per cent of a lot. James Fergus had done his usual news broadcast on both Wednesday and Thursday evenings and had, as usual, gone out for a drink or two after each. He might have killed Amanda before his newscast and Barnes after it.

Nothing had been found out about the present whereabouts of Byron Kingsley or about the friends with whom he had gone to wherever he had gone. Bill Weigand, sitting in his office in West Twentieth Street, waiting a break, waiting a hunch, had hardly supposed there would be—not yet. Nor did he suppose that Byron Kingsley, a man suddenly famous, much photographed, distinctive in appearance, would long be missing. . . . Amanda Towne's brother had flown in from Seattle, and had said he had no idea who inherited Amanda's money and that he didn't, furthermore, give much of a damn and would they please leave him alone? . . . The State police of Arkansas were, as requested, trying to find out anything there was to be found out about one Carl Cunningham, and had so far discovered only that his resignation from the periphery of the State University faculty had been quite voluntary.

In short, the files grew—a monument heaped patiently over murder.

It was after five when the report came, by telephone (to be followed, in due course, by the stipulated report on the form prescribed), that a man giving the name Carl Cunningham had been a passenger on that day's 8:40 A.M flight of American Airlines to Little Rock, Arkansas. His name had not been on the original passenger list. He had gone to the airport on the chance, and picked up a "no show." (The "no show" had been one Arthur Knight.) The plane had some time since set down in Little Rock and the crew had scattered. So, at the moment, no further identification was possible. The "Carl Cunningham" of Flight 115 might well not be their Carl Cunningham. Nothing could be taken for granted.

Captain William Weigand is aware of this rule of police work, and in agreement with it. It is nevertheless often necessary to take certain things for granted, provisionally. He took for granted that Cunningham, their Cunningham, had returned to Little Rock. He notified the Little Rock police and the State police of Arkansas, asking open eyes.

Then he went home. . . .

"It doesn't sound as good now as it did when I first thought of it," Jerry North said, at a little after nine o'clock. They sat in the Weigands' living room and drank coffee, with the lights low in the room and the curtains drawn back on the big window which faced the river. The weather had worsened; an east wind drove a misty rain against the window, and the lights outside were blurred in the rain, seemed to flicker through the rain-washed glass. In the channel, vessels moved slowly, unhappily, and sounded sad horns.

Jerry, aided at intervals by Pam, had advanced his theory of collusion between Cunningham and Kingsley. Jerry had progressively lost faith in his theory as he advanced it.

"It sounds fine," Pam said, while Bill still looked thoughtfully at Jerry North and Dorian held her chin in a cupped hand and looked at him too. "Very ingenious."

No more than that, Jerry was afraid, and said so. An invention—not impossible, not even implausible. Merely a little too intricate, a little too devious, for life. But at that, Bill Weigand shook his head.

"We come across some honeys," he said. "A good deal more complicated than yours. It could have happened that way."

"Too neat," Jerry said, arguing now against himself.

"I don't," Bill said, "say it happened that way. But—" He paused, drank coffee, put his cup down.

"I think," Dorian said, "that it's like the shadow of what really happened. Distorted, somehow. Or, a picture made by a cloud. The picture is half in the mind. But the cloud is there."

"You think in shapes," Bill told her.

"Of course," she said. "How else? In shapes, and colors."

"All right," Pam said, "what is it a shadow of, then? A distortion of?"

"It's no good," Jerry said. "As a matter of fact, we don't know that Cunningham comes into it at all. Into murder. Into my bank account, yes. God yes. But—"

He stopped, because Bill Weigand shook his head at him. Bill said they knew—at least could strongly believe—that Carl Cunningham came into at least part of it, and that that part of it included Amanda Towne. Which was not to say that it included the death of Amanda Towne.

"You see," Bill told them, "Cunningham obviously entered her mind while her interview with Kingsley was pending. She asked people in Arkansas to find out about both of them, coupled them."

"She might," Pam said, "only have had Arkansas brought into her mind. Because Kingsley comes from there. And then thought, 'I wonder what ever happened to poor old Carl, who's down there some place.' And killed two birds with one stone."

Bill doubted it. He thought the connection more direct. He thought the connection came from the book.

"I—" he said, and then said, "Wait a minute." He went to the telephone, and talked and waited and talked again, and waited again. Finally he said, "Gray? Weigand," and listened, and said he was sorry and that what he had to ask would only take a minute.

"You said you read *Look Away, Stranger,*" Bill said. "And marked certain sections for Miss Towne to read. Because she wouldn't have time to read the whole book, and would need to show some familiarity with it. Do you remember what you marked?"

He said, "Oh, I don't expect page for page. Generally." As he listened once more, he held his fingers in the air and rubbed tips together. Dorian flowed out of her chair, found a pencil, and flowed back into it. Bill made notes on the telephone pad. Finally, he said, "Thanks," and then, "Right. If it turns out to be needed," and hung up.

"I'm sorry," Dorian said. "I was doing a double crostic. I forgot to put it back."

Bill grinned at her. He consulted his notes. He reported.

Tony Gray, in the course of preparing Amanda Towne for her interview, had read—at any rate, had skimmed—*Look Away, Stranger*. He had marked certain passages he thought would, in the time she had for reading, give Amanda the "general feel" of the book. One of the passages evidently, although Gray could not precisely remember the pages covered, had been the foggy description of "Carl Connington" in his swamp (or mountain?) cabin, haunted by demons of the past (or future?). There had been several other passages, later in the book. At least one of them had, also, been concerned with "Connington."

"We're safe," Bill said, "in thinking that it was the book which brought Cunningham to Miss Towne's mind, prompted her enquiries about him. Connected him with Kingsley, so they were coupled in her mind."

"Recognized him in the book," Bill Weigand repeated. "Yes, it could have been that." He nodded slowly. "It could have been that," he said again.

"And got killed," Pam said, "just as Jerry thought. Because if she let the cat out of the bag, Mr. Cunningham would have to sue." She paused. "Or was I the one who put that in?" she asked, of anybody who had an answer.

"You did, I think," Jerry said. "It's sometimes hard to tell."

Pam agreed with that. "Sometimes," she said, "we act like a mosaic." She considered. "I mean," she said, "where does one of us end off and the other begin? It's very nice, really."

There was a brief silence of agreement. Then Bill said that, if they settled on Cunningham, there was a simpler explanation, and one which did not so immediately involve Byron Kingsley.

"It's possible," Bill said, "that something in what she read tipped Miss Towne off to something else. Gave significance to something she remembered. Perhaps proved something to her that it wouldn't have proved to anyone else. About Cunningham."

"What?" Jerry said, and, with something like excitement in his voice, answered himself. "*That he was a murderer,*" Jerry said. "In real life, as in the book. Wait—in Chicago. In the old days. Is that what you mean?"

"It could have been that," Bill said. But there was something in the tone of his voice.

"You don't think it was that," Pam said, as a statement.

Bill smiled faintly. He said she jumped. As she so often jumped. He did not say it wasn't that.

"Your voice did," Pam told him.

He shook his head. He said, if that was true, his voice spoke out of turn. He did not reject murder to cover murder—murder uncovered, by some association in a woman's mind; murder to be covered up again.

"Only," he said, "there could be something even simpler. It rather leaps into the mind."

He looked at his wife, at Pam and Jerry North. There was

nothing in their faces to indicate their minds had been leaped into.

"I guess it doesn't," he said. "Well—" He shrugged slightly, as if in dismissal of a fancy. He spoke in a different tone. He asked Jerry whether he had heard anything of Byron Kingsley's whereabouts.

"No, damn it," Jerry said.

"Nor we," Bill said.

"I do hope," Pam said, "that nothing's happened to *him*." She looked at Jerry. "All right," she said, "even now."

She stretched the maternal instinct far, Jerry told her.

It was an hour later that the telephone rang. They had got no further; they had even drifted to other matters. International politics had momentarily diverted Jerry's mind from impending bankruptcy—personal bankruptcy, in any case. "No!" Dorian said, of the telephone. "Oh—*no*."

"Yes," Bill said, into the telephone. "Right. Put him on." There was a long pause. "Hello, sergeant," Bill said then, and the others sat silent, heard an indistinguishable scratching of words from the receiver. "The hell you say," Bill said, and, after a time, "No, I didn't." He listened again, briefly, to the scratching sound. "No," he said. "Not enough to go on." Again he listened. He said he appreciated that; said they would have to take a chance on that. He said, after listening again, "Thanks. It may come to that," and then replaced the receiver.

He looked at the others for a moment, and there was a puzzled expression on his face.

"Something's gone wrong," Dorian said. "Is that it, Bill?"

"I don't know," Bill said. "Something I didn't expect, I'll admit. Cunningham seems to have shown up. In Arkansas. At the cabin up in the hills. At least—"

At least, there was a light in the cabin, and smoke was rising from its chimney. The Arkansas State police had been keeping a general eye on the place, on request. It appeared that Cunningham had returned from his wanderings. Presuming it was he and, although he had not actually been seen, it could be presumed it was.

"Not a tramp?" Jerry said. "Somebody holing up for the night?"

Bill shook his head. There was more than that. The day before a letter had come for Cunningham, and that day another. He had not called for his mail, but it was evident that he had let somebody know in advance of his return.

"Why," Pam asked, "don't the police go up to the cabin and say, 'Mr. Cunningham, I presume?' "

"Because I asked them not to," Bill said. "We've nothing to hold him on, obviously. The police might—annoy him. Lead him to take off again. I don't want that."

"Bill," Dorian said, "don't tell me that—"

"I'm afraid so," Bill said. "I'm afraid I'll have to take a little trip. The inspector disposing."

They looked at him.

"Because," Bill said, "he oughtn't to be there. In fact—he oughtn't to be anywhere."

XII

THE CAB HAD TAKEN them almost home when Jerry broke a long silence to announce that he thought he, also, would take a little trip—the same trip Bill Weigand planned to take. There was, he said, no use sitting around worrying. He might as well see Carl Cunningham and find out. See Cunningham and, if necessary, grovel. It could do no harm.

"Phil wouldn't agree," Pam said.

Jerry supposed not. Phil viewed with a marked lack of enthusiasm the tendency of clients to rush into things without their hands in his. It was by such precipitate action clients got themselves into the troubles they expected Phil to get them out of. There was no use in having a lawyer if—

Jerry agreed. He had often said he agreed. But all the same, he was going to fly out—fly out on the morning plane Bill was taking, if he could get a seat—and ask Cunningham what he had in mind doing. Sometimes the personal approach helped; if Cunningham realized that North Books, Inc., was very, very sorry about everything, and most, most anxious to make amends, he might consent to leave North Books with its corporate shirt. Man to man, Jerry said, and cards on the table—and, of course, such gentle waving of the costs and uncertainties of litigation as might be appropriate.

"And Phil," Pam said. "We can always wave Phil. People think twice when we wave Phil at them."

The cab stopped. On new instructions, it started up again, backtracked toward the consolidated ticket office of the air lines. If Jerry wanted a seat—and to get a check taken in payment—personal appearance seemed best.

"Two seats," Pam said, and was looked at. "Two," she said.

Jerry had expected it. Pamela North's view of air travel is extremely dim. She regards encouraging reports on passenger miles safely flown as without personal application, pointing out that she is not a passenger mile and that, if she can help it, Jerry is not going to be either. What happens to airplanes, Pamela North believes, is that they fall down. If others think differently, let others fly. But not Jerry—at any rate, not alone.

"You know perfectly well," she said now, "that if you're going to take this awful chance, I'm going to take it with you. For better or—or airplanes. As we agreed. I'm not going to sit home beside myself. Two can die as cheaply as one."

"But—" Jerry said.

"It's no use," Pam said. "As you know perfectly well. Also, I'll wear my oldest clothes."

He blinked at that; he ran fingers through his hair.

"So Mr. Cunningham will see we can't afford a million," Pam said. "Or anything like it. We'll both grovel. Much more—"

"All right," Jerry said. There was no use arguing. Nor was he sure he wished to argue since, for him, all things are brighter when Pam shares them.

American Airlines could provide two seats on Flight 115, 8:40 A.M., for Little Rock, Arkansas. American Airlines, after talking it over with itself, and staring fixedly at credit cards, would accept a check, under the circumstances. The Norths drove home, through the rain.

It was raining Sunday morning, in the spiritless fashion so often characteristic of November rains. There was also fog. Pam was relieved. "They'll never fly in this," she told Jerry as a cab took them toward LaGuardia. "Thank goodness. Even they will know better."

But "they" did not. American Airlines Flight 115 was loading in a manner entirely matter of fact—quite as if it were routine to plunge through a light fog, and a light rain, into a dark, unwelcoming sky. They must be crazy, Pam thought, and sat beside Jerry in a comfortable seat, and held Jerry's hand with uncomfortable vigor. And *we* must be. And where is Bill?

The big plane filled, and Bill was not among those who filled it. "Something's happened," Pam told Jerry. "Probably Cunningham has turned up some place else. We ought to get out of this thing right now and—"

Bill Weigand came into the plane. The door of the plane was closed behind Bill Weigand. Bill Weigand came down the aisle and looked at them. "What the—?" Bill said, and the stewardess said, "Fasten your seat belts, please," and an electric sign said, in red, the same thing. Another sign said, "No Smoking." Bill shook his head, and sat in a seat some distance down the aisle, and fastened his seat belt, and shook his head again. And the plane began to move.

"Ouch," Jerry said. "Your ring's digging in."

"What a thing to say," Pam said. "In our last moment. Just before—just before we're burned alive. Or—"

The plane stopped. Laboriously, after a few minutes, it turned around. Then it did nothing.

"Also," Pam said, "we're heading in the wrong direction. Little Rock is west of New York. Or, we're on the wrong plane. This one's going to Europe. And—"

The plane started up, taking off into the northeasterly wind. Pam closed her eyes. She didn't want to see it happen. Just let it happen—all at once, without warning. It was the best way. One moment you were alive and the next—

The plane moved faster, and made more noise. Then it moved in a different fashion. Pam reached out and took Jerry's other hand. She wanted to tell him how fine it had been, always, and how glad she was that, if it had to be this way, it would be both of them and— But she could not make her stiff lips move. So he would never know—never know how fine it had all been, or any of the things she had never remembered to tell him, because no matter how close you are to another person, there is never time to remember everything and—

"Why," Pam North said, in a quite normal tone. "It's cleared up. How sudden. It's as if—" She looked out the window. Looked into sunshine; looked down at heaped, white softness, with sunshine on it. "We must," Pam said, "be up. Quite a way up."

"And," Bill Weigand said, standing beside them, "what are you two doing here?"

"Praying," Pam said. "In a manner of speaking."

Jerry told Bill Weigand what they were doing there and Bill made a sound which, it seemed to Pam, expressed doubt or, at the least, considerable reservation. But, in words, he said only that he was glad Inspector O'Malley had not known in advance that the Norths, also, were flying west. Even without this knowledge, O'Malley had needed to be persuaded, it being his simple and direct theory that, if Weigand wanted Cunningham, and thought he had something on Cunningham, he should have him picked up and sent back. Told that it was not yet that simple, he snorted mildly and pointed out that wishy-washiness was growing on Weigand, doubtless because of his continued association with the Norths. But, not knowing that the Norths were going too, Inspector O'Malley had in the end authorized, only hoping that Weigand knew what he was doing.

The big DC-6 glittered its way west in sunshine. After a time there were no clouds below them, and the earth—the tiny earth—could be seen far below. It was, Pam thought, much neater from this distance—tiny fields regular as small green napkins, hilly country simplified, only threadlike roads still, for the most part, meandering to what appeared little purpose. "See?" Pam said, looking down. "It doesn't really matter which road one takes, because they all join up again. We must remember that next time we drive some place."

For three hours the diminished earth rolled under them and then, with cheerful matter-of-factness, the stewardess served lunch—served consommé, and veal sauté and broccoli, and french pastry and coffee. That, rushing through nothing, with peril on every side—and especially below—so pleasant a lunch should be so lightheartedly served (to so many people, too) struck Pam North as, in a fashion, preposterous. A triumph of the human spirit, Pam thought; a gallant gesture in the face of catastrophe. Those who dress for dinner in lion-infested jungles have nothing on us, Pam thought, and nibbled veal—and wondered, unexpectedly, just how they did it. Frivolous, Pam thought, and finished pastry and coffee. The condemned woman ate a reasonably hearty meal.

They had just finished when the airplane started to slant down toward the distant earth. Then Memphis—a stewardess identified it as Memphis—began to rush up at them. They fastened seat belts again, and put out cigarettes and then the airplane started to tip over. Pam closed her eyes with that, and held on to both Jerry's hands and—thought frantically, once again, that she had let time slip through her fingers, and had not told Jerry all the things she had, in their years (now about to end), not remembered to tell him. But then the airplane landed, gently, and shuffled across the airfield, rather like a great goose, and stopped and the door was opened.

They had almost half an hour to walk on solid pavement, stretching their legs. Looking at Pam, Jerry took her arm and held it, since she might, he thought, run to stretch hers. But she did not, and they got back on the airplane—which now had fewer passengers, and some of them strangers—and went up again. It was not quite so bad as before. Pam kept her eyes open long enough to see that they were about to run into some gigantic trees. She closed her eyes then, and stiffened, and waited—and they cleared the trees by some hundreds of feet. They did not go so high, this time (so that the earth was much nearer and, as a result, looked much harder) and it seemed that they had hardly got into the air before they started to come down out of it, and once more to tip over—call it "banking" if you wanted to, but it was a kind of tipping over—and they fastened seat belts again. But Pam kept her eyes open, and was only a little paralyzed. Perhaps, Pam North thought, I can become a passenger mile, after all.

It was early afternoon in Little Rock, and a State trooper met the airplane—met it with a car for Weigand, and a road map and a look of mild surprise when Weigand introduced the Norths, as fellow members of the expedition. He said that the country around Top Town was sort of rough-like for a lady. He said that, at last report, Cunningham—or somebody, anyhow—was still in the cabin on the hill, and that the postmaster at Top Town had instructions to get in touch if he came down out of it for his mail, or for provisions. And instructions not to tell Cunningham that the State police had expressed interest in him.

"Right," Bill said. "We want to talk to him. Don't want him to get scared and run."

The trooper's expression was that of a man who doesn't get it, and whose business it isn't. The car provided was a police car, although it did not look it. It had two-way radio, so if Weigand wanted help he could ask for it. He would have to remember that there weren't many of them—there are never enough policemen anywhere, as any policeman will agree—and that help might take a time to get to them. Especially on the roads they would find up around Top Town.

Bill said, "Right," and that he appreciated everything, and the trooper unhooked his motorcycle from the tow hitch on the back of the car and went off on it. Bill and the Norths found the road out of Little Rock—a road the map showed clearly; a road which would take them into the Boston Mountains, and to Harrison, Arkansas, near the State line in the north and, if they stayed on it long enough, to Springfield, Missouri. A hundred and forty miles to Harrison, and something less to the back road which would lead them to Top Town.

It was much warmer in Arkansas than it had been in New York and, at first, much dryer. They went through rolling country as they went north, the road turning between hills. But, consistently, they climbed and the hills grew higher. Summer still seemed to cling to the valleys, even where the hills shadowed them. But after an hour, clouds began to build up in the west and, very suddenly, the low November sun went behind the clouds. Then, almost at once, dusk spread through the valleys. It was only a little after four when Weigand switched on the car lights.

They were halfway from Little Rock to Top Town, then, and the road was climbing more sharply, descending more abruptly, twisting between increasingly more precipitous hills. They climbed a long way up and then, in the dusk, there were hills all around them, and narrow valleys, with streams running through them. The road surface was good, but it was a mountain road now, and not a road for speed. (Yet some cars, bearing Arkansas licenses, seemed unperturbed by steepness and sharp curves, and went up and down and around with impetuous confidence.)

"We are," Pam said, "a long way from anywhere, aren't we?"

Lights began to come on in houses they drove past.

"It is the saddest time of day," Pam said. "Unless you're going home. See all the people who are at home?"

She was sitting between them. Jerry put an arm around her.

They had gone a hundred miles by five-thirty, and it was then quite dark. The lights bored through darkness; on curves the lights shot off willfully, lighting the tops of valley trees. Bill pulled off at a tiny town for gas and Jerry lifted his arm down and found it heavy and powerless. He shook it and it tingled, while a man in overalls filled the tank, and said that the turnoff for Top Town was about twenty miles ahead, and not very well marked, and to the right. He said that it wasn't much of a road, either, and that they'd have ten miles of it, and that it looked like rain. He said that if it rained much, the road to Top Town would be pretty tough going for a car like this one. Having thus cheered everyone, he said it would be five dollars and twenty-four cents.

Jerry drove when they started up again. After five miles, rain began. It was not a heavy rain, but it was the kind of rain which tends to its knitting. The rain skittered in the headlight beams, and the windshield wipers went methodically back and forth, and they were miles from anywhere in a small dark box.

"I'm not sure," Pam said, "that this was such a very good idea."

They churned on, through rain, hemmed in by hills. "Probably," Pam said, "this would be very beautiful, if we could see it," and then, "I'm just talking to keep our spirits up."

"Mine soar," Jerry told her, going very carefully around a corner, with the lights staring straight ahead, fixed and unco-operative. "We've gone about eighteen."

They went another two. No road went off to the right. "He only said 'about,'" Pam said, reassuring, "and even when people say 'exactly' they usually mean 'about.'"

They had gone twenty-four miles from the filling station when Bill said, "Take it easy," and shot a flashlight beam at the road's edge. The beam picked up a wooden sign, a dejectedly sagging sign. Jerry stopped by it. It was a wedge at one end and, dimly, it said, "Top Town. Ten miles." The road it pointed to was not immediately apparent. Then it was. It was a dirt road and water streamed on it, and it plunged down from the main road. Bill shone his light down the plunging road. At the bottom of its drop there was what appeared to be a bridge. Above that the road seemed to rise straight up.

The turn was at right angles. Jerry cut hard, and inched into the narrow road. The car skidded momentarily, and Jerry caught it out of its skid, and they crept down. They crept across the bridge, and loose planking banged under the car and the bridge perceptibly shook. They started on up the other side, and did not go straight up, but near enough, on a road built to the width of one car only, and with a sharp turn at the top of its first rise. The headlights shot up into the air, so that at the crest the road appeared not so much to turn as to vanish.

They crept up and around, and beyond there was another rise. They went on. Now and then the wheels slipped a little, spun a little on the slippery surface. Once they spun toward the side of the road, perilously—there was a ditch at the side of the road, and beyond it a steep pitch downward. But Jerry caught the car, and eased it on, and the wheels found traction. "Whew!" Jerry said, and went again, cautiously, up and around. And up and around, and up and over, in a twisting tunnel between trees—a thousand miles from anywhere, in the blackest of darkness. Here, on this road to Top Town—this road to nowhere—

there were no reassuring lights in houses. Nobody, evidently, lived here, or near here, or ever had or ever would.

"It is," Pam North said, "all very unreal, isn't it?"

It was, and yet, real enough—real enough to Jerry, nursing the car upward; real enough to Bill Weigand, who felt urgency tightening in him, and impatience. They went four miles, and five, and always up and around, and if they met a car coming toward them it was inconceivable that any solution would arise, ever. The cars, Pam thought, would merely stand, glaring at each other, into infinity. They went six miles and seven and eight and around another curve, and almost missed Top Town, which was a place where the road widened, grudgingly; which was a two-story frame building, with an unrailed, high porch, and wooden steps leading up to it—which was a sign across the front of the building which read, "Perkins General Store," and a smaller sign which read, "U. S. Post Office. Top Town, Arkansas."

Jerry pulled the car up parallel to the porch. And then they could see, through a window—a window made almost opaque by grime—a single light burning inside the store. There was no sign of life in the store. Bill Weigand got out and climbed the wooden steps, his feet falling heavily on them, and crossed the porch and knocked at a closed door. It sounded as if he had knocked on a wooden drum. Nothing happened and he knocked again. Then another light came on in the building, and a man's voice was loud—loud and, seemingly, angry. "Give a man time, can't you?" the voice demanded.

Bill gave the man time. They could hear the man walking inside the building on a wooden floor, and it was as if he walked on a drum. Then the door opened.

The man was tall and thin; he wore overalls and a woolen shirt. He had long white hair which lay flat on his head, and fell straight down the back of his neck. He said, "Well? Want something?"

"Mr. Perkins?" Bill said.

"Suppose I am?"

"I'm looking for Carl Cunningham," Bill told him. "The State police—"

"So you're the one, air you?" He looked beyond Bill, at the car. "Who're those other folks?"

"Friends of mine," Bill said. "I'm a policeman. From New York."

"Fars I know," the white-haired man said, "Cunningham's up at that shack of Nelson's. Got mail here for him. He done something bad, I reckon?"

"I want to talk to him," Bill said. "Can you tell me how to get to this shack?"

"Reckon maybe," the man said. "Want to come in? You and these friends of yours? So as a person can get a look at you?"

They went in. The room was long and dusty; there was a counter along one side, and cans and packaged food on shelves behind it, and part of a cheese under a dusty glass cover, and at one end of the room there was an iron stove. Two lights dangled from cords and fought halfheartedly against darkness. And a shotgun leaned against the counter.

The tall old man looked at them; he looked longer at Pam than at the men and said, "City people, ain't you?" His question was, apparently, directed to Pam.

"Yes," she said. "I'm afraid so Mr.—Mr. Perkins?"

"Talk like a furriner," the man said. "Who'd I be if not Perkins?"

"Well," Pam said, "that's a little hard to say, isn't it? Almost anybody, probably. Are you Mr. Perkins?"

"Told you I was," he said. "So you want to see Carl?"

"Yes," Bill said. "You say he's back in the cabin? Whatever it is?"

"Ain't seen him," Perkins said. "Like I told the troopers. Somebody's up there. Place up the road a piece you can see a light, when there's a light. Was last night. That's all I know."

"You didn't go up to see?"

"What'd I do that for? He wants his mail, he knows where it is. You figuring on going up there? The lady too?"

"Well—" Jerry said, and Pam looked at him, looked around the store quickly, shook her head briefly.

"Yes," Pam said, again.

"Never make it," Perkins said. "Not in those city shoes, ma'am. If you call them shoes."

Pam looked at her feet. Abercrombie and Fitch had called them shoes; called them walking shoes. It was true that Madison Avenue was very far away.

"How far is it?" Bill asked.

"Two-three miles," Perkins said. "You drive up the road a piece and there's a place you can pull off, if you don't miss it. On the right-hand side. That's where the path starts. About a mile up the hill, the shack is. Lady'll never make it. Not in those shoes."

"The lady'll make it, Mr. Perkins," Pam said. "She'll— Wait. Haven't you got shoes for sale?"

"Reckon," Perkins said. "Sneakers." He looked at her feet. "Boy's size, maybe," he said, and turned away, and went to the far end of the big room and began to rummage. After some time he came back, carrying a pair of dusty tennis shoes. He said, "Smallest I've got," and handed them to Pam. Pam sat on a box, which seemed to be the only thing to sit on, and put the shoes on. Her feet slid around in the shoes. Still—

She nodded to Jerry, who got out money.

"Two-three miles," Perkins said again, being asked again. "Room to pull off—only place along there there is. Path goes straight up outa there. Can't miss it, hardly."

They went toward the door and Perkins watched them. Pam's city feet slapped in too large shoes. She carried what she, together with Abercrombie and Fitch, had previously regarded as walking shoes. When they went out on the porch, thunder rolled in the hills. But Pam said, "For goodness' sake! *Look!*" and pointed upward.

Clouds hurried across the sky. But it seemed, rather, as if a full moon rode through the sky, picking its white and brilliant path among dark clouds.

Perkins came to the door and stood looking out at them.

"Could be," he said, "you'll get stuck down there. Lot uh rain last few days. Want to watch it."

"We'll watch it," Bill promised him, and this time he got behind the wheel. He drove very slowly on the narrow road, which here ran straight, and downhill. They crept along, and Jerry held a flashlight ready. But when the moon escaped from the clouds, it paled even the car headlights.

They had gone only half a mile or so when, from ahead and, it seemed, above them there was the sharp crack of a shot. In a second there was another, and then, rapidly, two more.

"For heaven's sake," Pam said. "Feudin'?"

"More likely hunting," Jerry said. "Don't they hunt coons at night?"

Bill Weigand did not give a theory. But he drove faster on the narrow, slippery road. Then, after they had gone a little more than three miles from the general store, he checked speed suddenly, and the car tried to skid, and was caught out of it.

The car lights picked up the dark shape of another car, parked off the road, on the right.

The car was motionless, unlighted.

Very cautiously, Bill nosed the police car up behind it. There was not quite room to get the police car off the road before its bumper nosed into the rear bumper of the empty car. Bill gave a little more gas, trying to push in, but the wheels spun. He cut the motor.

"End of the line," he said. "I suppose this is the—"

There was the sound of another shot. It came, now, from above them.

"Sit tight," Bill said, and didn't himself, but went out quickly to the road. "Come this way," he told them, and Pam, and Jerry after her, slid under the wheel and joined him on the road, with the car between them and the steep rise of a hill which climbed from the roadway.

The moon came out full, then, and bathed the hillside. In front of the car which had been parked there was a break in undergrowth—a narrow break, in the moonlight only a shadow.

"The path," Pam said and started toward it and said, "*Damn!*" and stopped, perilously, on one foot. "Shoe came off," she said, and reached for Jerry to steady herself while, with toes, she fished in mud for a tennis shoe. She found it and wriggled foot into it. "All right now," she said, "I guess," and put both feet on the ground and began to shuffle forward. But then Bill Weigand said, in a low, sharp voice, "*Wait, Pam!*"

She turned toward him.

"Listen," he said, and now in a whisper.

They listened. There was the sound of movement—hurried movement. It came from up the path—up the steep side of the hill. Someone scrambled on the path, and the sound came closer.

Bill Weigand got a revolver out of a shoulder holster and the barrel was bright in the moonlight. He moved forward, beyond the car which had stopped them, until, with gun ready, he faced the path. Pam and Jerry started after him, and Bill jerked his head quickly in negation, and they stopped, screened by the two cars.

The scrambling sound came down toward them. And the scrambler came in sight—lunging down the path, as if running down the path. He was a big man in the moonlight. He grabbed at branches, at shrubs, steadying himself, and came fast.

They saw Bill hold his revolver ready, then saw him lower it.

Byron Kingsley lunged the last few feet down the path, and leaped a ditch and stood in front of Bill Weigand, his breath coming fast.

"Good," he said. "Hoped it was you. Saw the lights from up there."

He waved back up the hillside.

"He's gone—" Kingsley began, and then Pam and Jerry moved up from behind the cars which had obscured them. Kingsley stared at them for an instant.

"*My God,*" he said. "You here, Mr. North? And you, ma'am?"

"Yes," Jerry said. "That's right, Kingsley."

His voice grated in his own ears. That was fine with him. He felt like grating.

Kingsley looked at him, and seemed surprised. But after an instant he turned back to Weigand.

"Looks like you're going to need that, "he said, and looked at the gun Bill held. "He's gone—he's gone crazy. Starts shooting when he sees anybody. Doesn't matter who he sees, I guess."

"We heard shots," Bill said, and his voice was quiet. "Was he shooting at you?"

"Rifle," Kingsley said. "I tell you, he's gone crazy. All I wanted was—to help him, I guess. Let him—" He broke off. "I guess it doesn't matter much now, does it? Guess nobody can help him."

"You're talking about Cunningham," Bill said, without enquiry in his voice.

"Sure," Kingsley said. He talked now in a low voice, as Bill Weigand had. "Followed him out here to—" Again he stopped. "Well," he said, "he's a friend of mine. Wanted to give him a chance to—" Once more he stopped, and shook his handsome head. His tawny hair was bright in the moonlight.

"Followed him out here?" Bill said. "From New York?"

"Yes," Kingsley said. "What are we going to do? I tell you, he's gone crazy. Shooting that damn rifle every time—well, every time anything moves, I guess."

Bill nodded his head. He said, "How did you know he had come out here, Mr. Kingsley?"

Kingsley made an impatient movement—a movement which said that this was no time for that. But Bill waited; obviously waited. He seemed now entirely unhurried.

"Saw him," Kingsley said. "At the airport. I was going south for a couple of days with some friends. Saw him getting on a plane. Checked and found the plane went to Little Rock. Wasn't any doubt this time it was Carl. That was yesterday morning."

"Right," Bill said. "And you followed him?"

"Listen," Kingsley said. "Sure I did. Took the afternoon

plane. Give him a chance to—" He stopped and shook his head again.

"Because," Bill said, "you thought he'd killed Miss Towne? And her husband?"

"All right," Kingsley said. "Why are *you* here, sir?"

"Right," Bill Weigand said. "Did you just get here, Mr. Kingsley?"

He hadn't, Kingsley said, and there was impatience in his voice—impatience at wasted time. "We stand here talking?" he asked and Bill Weigand shook his head, and said not for long. And waited.

Kingsley had, he said, stayed overnight at Little Rock. Come up that morning. Climbed up to the cabin and found nobody there and waited around a while and driven into Harrison for lunch and come back. It had been raining hard—"hell of a storm in Harrison"—when he got back to the foot of the hill, and he had waited in the car until the rain let up and then climbed the path. It had been just dusk. He had seen Cunningham in front of the cabin. Cunningham was carrying a rifle. He had shouted at him—shouted, "Hey, *Carl!*" Cunningham had turned around and looked, Kingsley said, for the source of the shout, and then Kingsley had shouted his name.

"He yelled, '*Go away!*'" Kingsley told them. "And shook the gun. I tried to argue with him, but he went into the cabin. I could just make him out inside, by the window, with that damn gun. Sorry, ma'am."

Kingsley had, he said, decided to wait until it was fully dark. "I don't," he said, "know just what I planned. Except I wanted to—to make him see that this wasn't getting him anywhere. Hell —Carl's damn near—damn near like a daddy to me."

It had started to rain again, and Kingsley waited in the rain, hidden in the trees. Then the rain stopped and the moon showed through and he had moved—and then Cunningham had started shooting at him. He had dodged behind trees and then, looking down toward the road—a mile from him, hundreds of feet below him—he had seen the lights of a car moving along the road.

He had thought he would get down to it and stop it and try to get help, and had run for the path, and then Cunningham had fired again, several times. And missed, but once not by much.

"We've got to get him somehow," Kingsley said. "We can't just stand here talking."

"No," Bill Weigand said, and to Pam it seemed that there was uncertainty in his tone—an uncertainty she had never heard in his voice before. "Have you any plan, Mr. Kingsley?"

And that, too, was unlike Bill, Pam thought—very unlike Bill Weigand, who does not pass the buck. Or, who never had before.

"I don't—" Kingsley began, and then snapped his fingers. "There's another path," he said. "Goes around the hill, sort of. Easier, but a good deal longer. Comes out more or less behind the cabin. If I went that way and you gave me a start—ten minutes maybe—and then came up I could—well distract him."

"You've got a gun?" Weigand asked. "A revolver?"

Kingsley shook his head. But he could—oh, yell at Cunningham from the far side of the cabin. Show himself—get Cunningham to that side. Then Weigand, timing himself by the shout, would have a chance to rush the—"the poor crazy old guy." Would that work?

"It might," Bill said. "All right, Kingsley."

"Mrs. North had better stay here," Kingsley said. "No sense in her—"

"No," Pam said. "Here alone? Miles from anywhere? And with a crazy man running loose? Suppose he gets past you and comes down here to get the car and—no. I don't stay here."

"Then," Kingsley said, "come with me. It's an easy path, as they go around here."

"Well—" Pam said, and looked at the path which wasn't easier. It appeared to go straight up. "Well—"

"No," Bill said. "Mrs. North had better stay with us. You go ahead, Kingsley. Ten minutes?"

"About," Kingsley said. "Make it fifteen. O.K.?"

"Right," Bill said. "Be careful."

Kingsley went. He went straight up the straight-up path, but only for fifty feet or so, and they could watch him in the moonlight, which now was clear, unwavering. Then he went off, toward the right.

"*Bill!*" Pam said. "You—you *let* him. By himself, without a gun. Go to be—be *shot at!* How—" She stopped and shook her head.

Bill Weigand turned to her. The moonlight was full on his face and he smiled slightly. A—a conciliating smile? Why, Pam thought—*Bill Weigand.* After all these years.

"I imagine," Bill said, "that Mr. Kingsley will make out all right. Cunningham doesn't seem to be much of a shot."

"Then why—" Pam began and thought, What's the use, and then, It's dreadful to find this out about Bill. I can't believe— She looked away from Bill Weigand. She looked at Jerry, and Jerry was looking at Bill, and the expression on Jerry's face was one she could not quite fathom, although she had supposed that no expression on Jerry's face would ever baffle her.

They waited, and Pam felt very much alone. It seemed that they waited much longer than fifteen minutes, but finally Bill said, "Right," and started toward the path, his gun ready. At least, Pam thought, he goes first, even if he's—if he's— She would not, even in her mind, use the word. Not after so many years.

Pam went next, with Jerry behind. "To push," she explained. At least, that would be all right for the start. Later, if Jerry wanted to be brave and get in front of her. But, just now, pushing was more important.

It proved to be, as they climbed the path—which was in some places not a path at all, but only a place to scramble. Jerry pushed a good deal, and Pam kept losing the tennis shoes and finding them again. But Bill stopped each time and waited, and seemed in no hurry—seemed, on the other hand, almost reluctant, and very cautious and kept his revolver ready in his right hand, although its presence impeded him. It was a path which needed hands free, to pull with. It was a path which, at its worst, was only the suggestion of a path. And grass and dirt were wet under foot.

They could not see, at any moment, more than a few feet ahead, and after fifteen minutes it seemed to Pam that they had been climbing the hillside for hours. After another ten, she quit thinking about anything—anything except the next toiling, impossible, step. She should have taken the easier path with Byron Kingsley. Why had Bill then (and at no other time) shown firmness? She might better have stayed in the car. She might, come to that, better have stayed in New York. Then her muscles would not be wrenched so, nor her mind so wrenched—so pained —by what Bill Weigand had revealed about himself.

There was the sharp crack of a shot and, at what seemed the same instant, an angry whining sound above them. With almost no interval, there was a second brittle crack, and another whining.

"Down," Bill said, without turning, and Pam dropped to her knees, hugged against the rising earth. She could feel, without seeing, that Jerry went down behind her. But Bill stood, with his gun lifted, and only moved a little to one side, just off the path, behind a tree. They waited. Then Bill fired, Pam thought into the air. Almost instantly the rifle above them cracked again.

"All right," Bill said. "Come on," and started to walk on up the path. It seemed that the sound of the shots had given him cause to hurry toward them. As if the shots summoned him.

Abruptly, after a last lunge upward, the path opened out into a clearing. There was a small cabin in the clearing, hemmed by trees. It was the top of the hill; there was no more hill.

The cabin was dark in the moonlight, and there was no one in sight. But then, from behind it, the rifle cracked again, and again twice.

They had heard no shout—something had gone wrong there. But Kingsley had done what he promised. That was clear. He had come up behind the cabin, was making himself a target for the man inside the cabin—the "crazy" man who was shooting at anything that moved.

Bill ran then—ran across the clearing toward the cabin, the moon glinting on the revolver he held ready, but did not fire.

As he ran, someone shouted from behind the cabin. The words came clearly—

"*Carl!* No—watch it, man! *Watch it!*" There was the sound of someone running. And then, in a kind of wail, "Oh—my God. *My God!*"

And there was silence, then, except for the sound of Bill Weigand's running. It seemed that he was running on a treadmill—but the treadmill was the treadmill of time. Pam ran after him, then, and Jerry beside her, holding her. She lost both shoes and ran in stockinged feet on rough stubble, and did not feel the stubble.

They followed Bill around the cabin. Bill ran toward a tall man standing at the other side of the clearing—standing looking down, his big body slumped, his hands dangling.

Bill stopped beside him—stopped with a curiously abrupt movement and stood, also, looking down at something.

Pam and Jerry slowed, joined the other two.

They were looking down the side of a cliff—looking down to where, fifty feet below, a river dashed turbulently, dark and angry under the white light of the moon.

"I tried to stop him," Kingsley said. "He—he rushed at me. Fired a couple of times and then rushed. I guess he must have run out of cartridges. He—I dodged and he just—just went on. I yelled at him. You heard me yell at him?"

"Yes," Bill said. "We heard you."

"He just—ran over the edge. Didn't—didn't even scream. You'd have thought he'd have screamed when he began to fall. Wouldn't you have thought that?"

"Yes," Bill said. "I'd have thought that."

"God knows," Kingsley said. "He'd never have a chance in that." He pointed down at the swollen, racing river. "Chances are we'll never even—find him."

"Oh," Bill said, "I think we'll find his body, Mr. Kingsley.

Wherever you buried him. Three years ago, wasn't it? And probably—"

Byron Kingsley's hand shot toward his right hip. But he was not quick enough. Standing very close, Bill Weigand slapped the barrel of his revolver against the side of the big man's jaw. Kingsley went down.

Bill knelt beside him for a moment, and then stood up.

"Good," he said, as if to himself. "Didn't even break his jaw." He looked at Pam and Jerry, and Pam's eyes were wide with shock, with surprise.

"Of course," Bill said, "Cunningham's been dead for years. He'll be a skeleton by now—a long skeleton, I'd think. Jerry. You know how to call on the police radio?"

Jerry nodded. His eyes, too, showed shocked surprise.

"Then," Bill said, "do you mind sliding down and calling our friends? Because this"—he indicated the unconscious Byron Kingsley, Jerry North's beautiful author—"is a bit too heavy for the three of us to carry down."

XIII

Being told that she had put her finger on it, Pam North shook a doubtful head. On being told when, with what selection of words, she said, "But—I didn't mean that. I meant—"

Bill Weigand said he knew what she had meant. And that it was then—precisely then—that it had come together in his mind. She had, admittedly, said more than she meant.

"In all innocence," Pam told him. "In all ignorance, too. It never crossed my mind. So far as I know, it never even crossed my subconscious. It's still hard to believe."

The maternal instinct, Jerry told her, certainly died hard, once aroused. She would have, in the future, to keep an eye on it.

They were in the station restaurant in Little Rock, with only fifteen minutes to wait for the Norths' train to St. Louis. Pam had been firm about trains—nothing, she is convinced, happens on trains, or to them. When trains go around curves, they do not do it by tipping over.

Bill had been late in joining them; for a time it appeared that he would not arrive in time, which would have meant inevitably, that they would wait for another train, since loose ends must be tied together. It was true that Byron Kingsley was not a loose end. He was not loose anywhere, but tight in the Boone County jail. Nevertheless—

Bill said he was sorry to hold them up, and ordered coffee. He looked tired, but reasonably contented. He had spent most of the night watching some men digging in the clearing around the cabin above Mr. Perkins's store in Top Town, and watching other men fishing in the turbulent stream below the cabin. The men who fished had found a rifle. The men who dug had found a skeleton—the long skeleton of what had been a long man; the skeleton of what had been a man named Carl Cunningham. A dentist in Fayetteville had looked at photographs, looked at charts, and been certain of that. A physician in Chicago had looked at photographs, including those made many years before of a fracture of the tibia, and been reasonably certain of that.

There was a hole in the frontal bone of the skull and when the skeleton was lifted carefully out of a shallow grave a bullet had rattled in the skull. So that was that—and another thing for Byron Kingsley to deny. Which, in a minimum of words, he did, as he denied everything else—that he had smothered Amanda Towne and crushed the head of Russell Barnes; posed as Cunningham at the New York hotel and on the plane, fired rifle shots at Bill Weigand and Pam and Jerry North.

"Not," Bill said, "that he expected to hit us. Probably couldn't even see us. But to establish that Cunningham was alive and shooting. He started shooting when he saw the car lights, on the chance that I was in the car, coming to talk to Cunningham. Got up ahead of us and fired a few more, and then played out his little scene behind the cabin."

All of which, Byron Kingsley denied, and that he had killed anybody. Cunningham had been alive and done the shooting; Cunningham had fallen in the river and been swept away. The skeleton was that of someone else. It had to be.

Would he be tried for killing Cunningham? Or for the murders in New York? It was hard to say; it would be a matter for lawyers; for grand jurymen. It would depend, to some degree, on what evidence could be dug up, now that they knew—in New York and in Arkansas—what to dig for. But that is almost always the way of it, when no confession is offered. You know first, then you dig up proof of what you know.

Jerry looked at his watch. He compared it with the station clock. It was then that they had fifteen minutes left for the tying of loose ends.

"Pam put her finger on it," he said, promptingly.

"Right," Bill said. "She said Miss Towne had 'recognized' Cunningham in the book. Meaning she had recognized him as a character in the book, as you had. I'd been groping toward something. That brought it together. If she recognized Cunningham not only as a character but *as the author too,* there it was. Clear as clear. Then it all fitted.

"Perhaps it was the way he wrote—certain turns of phrase. Perhaps it was more than that. Cunningham had talked to her a lot, according to Fergus, about his plans to write. He may have outlined to her, years ago, the book he planned to write—and wrote on for years. Authors do talk about books they're going to write? And, sometimes write themselves into them?"

"God yes," Jerry North said, simply.

"She read part of *Look Away, Stranger,*" Bill said. "Perhaps read all of it. And became convinced that Cunningham was the author, not Kingsley. Let Kingsley see what she suspected that night in her suite. Probably said she was going to break it on her TV show. Perhaps asked him what he was going to do about it. And—found out."

"And her husband? Poor Mr. Barnes?"

"At a guess, Pam, she'd talked about it with Barnes. Said something like 'Read this and see if it hits you the way it does me.' And told Kingsley it wasn't her idea only. That somebody else would say the same thing. And—told him who."

"Look," Jerry said. "He killed Cunningham to get the book? So he could get it published as his own?"

That was possible, of course. Bill rather doubted it. It seemed more likely that Kingsley's first murder had been otherwise motivated, and about the motives they could only guess. It might have been that he had merely killed Cunningham in a brawl. Conceivably, even, he might have killed him by accident. But when, after burying Cunningham three years ago, he had left the cabin, he had taken the bulky manuscript of *Look Away, Stranger* with him. He had read it and, they could assume, been impressed. He had waited. When nothing happened, he had taken a chance—put his own name on the manuscript and started sending it around, probably hoping no more than that he could pick up a few dollars.

"He took a chance," Jerry said. "Cunningham might have shown the book to someone else."

There had been that chance, obviously. But Cunningham was a recluse. It was possible, also, that he had told Kingsley that nobody had seen the book. Perhaps he had even let Kingsley read the book, and had told him nobody else had. They could only guess. Probably, on that detail, they would never be able to do anything but guess.

"Five minutes," Jerry said, and put a bill down on the restaurant check.

"Killed Amanda Towne," Pam said. "Started to leave the suite and saw the maid working up the corridor. Thought she would find the body too soon after he was known to have been there. I suppose others knew he had the appointment? That Mrs. Fleming? Or that Mr. Gray?"

"Gray," Bill said.

"Moved the body from her suite to ours," Pam said. "Planted the lipstick mark on the pillow. Bill—was it just a coincidence that it was our suite?"

To a degree, Bill told them, as they stood up—to a degree it had to be. Kingsley had had no way of knowing they would be at the hotel. But—and here again Bill admitted he was guessing—Kingsley may well have seen them leaving their suite when they went out to dinner; seen them and recognized them. And carried Amanda Towne's body to their suite, instead of another, because their involvement would give him the chance to keep informed about what happened, and so in a position for such further improvisation as seemed desirable. As, for example, first seeking to implicate Judge Parkman; then switching to Cunningham.

"In other words," Pam said. "Straight men. From beginning to end, just straight men. That's us."

It was an odd way to describe Pamela North, Bill thought, as he walked with them to the train gate.

Dorothy Goodnow